SPONTANEOUS
GIGGLING

SPONTANEOUS GIGGLING

AND OTHER HUMAN GESTURES

31 Quick Stories

BEAR JACK GEBHARDT

Published by Seven Traditions Press

Bellvue, CO   London, UK   Singapore   Des Moines, IA.

This book is dedicated to

The *Boys' Night Out* Book Club

A Baker's Dozen of erudite chums who have been meeting for over thirty years. Thanks guys, for all the great reads, and even greater camaraderie. Ours is one of those gatherings that make life worth celebrating.

And to

Suzy Gebhardt

Again, because, among an infinite number of other reasons, she laughs at my jokes, says she loves my stories, and softly hums hymns while doing housework.

.

Table of Contents

Spontaneous Giggling

Table of Contents (cont.)

1

Spontaneous Giggling

Gladys' sudden explosive laughter startled Herbert. He looked up from the book he was reading— David McCullough's *The Pioneers, The Heroic Story of the Settlers who Brought the American Ideal West.*

Gladys had her ear buds in and was grinning at her Kindle.

Herbert was impressed with the courage of those pioneers who risked all, left all behind and explored new places. Those were the days, long gone.

Herbert and Gladys were sitting across the living room from each other on a cold December afternoon. They'd lived in this house for twenty-eight years. They'd moved in shortly after being married. Two more years it would be mortgage free. The fire in the gas fireplace was burning and Tips, their miniature poodle, was asleep on the couch, snuggled next to Gladys' thigh.

Herbert started to ask what was so funny but thought better of it. If he asked, which he might have to do several times before she heard him, she would pause her show or movie or clip by punching her screen , and then, removing one of her ear buds, she would explain what was so funny. Herbert was sure, having been here before, that whatever was so funny was funny to Gladys, but not readily shared with her longtime spouse.

Herbert went back to reading *The Pioneers*.

The phone—their landline—rang on the table next to Herbert's chair. This was an arrangement they'd made years ago, since Herbert seldom wore ear buds. With all the robo-calls coming in, Herbert seldom answered if it was a number he did not recognize. But this one looked vaguely familiar, even though no name was attached.

"Hello?"

"She's cheating you," a woman's voice said. "The sweet lady probably sitting across from you this instant, the bitch. She's cheating on you. And she's doing it with my husband, the bastard."

"Pardon?" Herbert said. "Who is this? What do you mean? What? Who is this?"

"Oh you'll find out soon enough," the woman said. "Everything's coming unraveled for these cheaters. You'll see. You'll see. Soon enough."

And then the caller hung up. Herbert was listening to a dial tone. He starred at the phone, pushed the button to hang up his end, looked over to Gladys, who was looking at him.

She punched her Kindle to put it on pause, and removed one ear bud.

"Who was that?" she asked.

Herbert shook his head. "Must have been a crank call."

"Why? What?"

"It was some lady, said you'd been cheating on me, with her husband."

"Louise said that? She knows? Louise called here? How did she..."

"Louise who?"

Suddenly, Gladys' jaw dropped, and her face took on a look of horrified surprise.

"Louise who?" Herbert asked again.

"I don't know. I mean, I was thinking of something else."

"Louise knows what?" Herbert asked.

Suddenly, Gladys' cell phone rang. It had been sitting on the couch next to her. She picked it up, looked at the number, and then to Herbert, held up one finger, the international signal to wait one moment while I answer this.

"Hello?" she said, and listened. Then, "Yes, yes. I don't know. Okay, yes, you're right. Okay. Finally .Okay."

"Who was that?" Herbert asked.

"Herbie, honey, we need to talk," Gladys said, setting down her phone, taking out her other ear bud and moving her kindle off her lap.

"What? What about? What do you mean?"

Gladys took a deep breath, let it out, clasped her hands and put them between her legs.

"I've met someone," Gladys said, quite calmly. "Who laughs at the same things I laugh at."

Gladys gave a spontaneous little giggle. Herbert frowned. "What are you giggling about?" he asked. She shrugged, and giggled again.

"At last," she said, "A new life. I'm free," and giggled yet once more, standing up to leave for a whole new life in unmapped, possibly dangerous but hopefully exciting and prosperous new territory.

2.

Fresh Air

At first, I thought Jimmy Fein didn't have much juice there between his ears, so I stayed away, didn't pay him much attention. In prison, someone who is not smart is dangerous to be around.

He was twenty or thirty years younger than me, in his late twenties, early thirties. I was fifty-five when convicted of insider trading and sentenced by the eighth judicial court to eight to ten in the federal pen. It was not a trivial sentence, nor a trivial sum I had garnered.

Since I'm an old guy, a first-timer and my crime was neither violent nor sexual nor glamorous nor brave, the young guys pretty much ignore me. To them, I'm boring. I present neither a threat nor a conquest. I have enough social mojo from my trading days to be able to call the bluff of young guys but I also recognize power when I see it.

In prison, the physical part of survival is fairly easy. After all, 98% of the men who go to prison don't die there. They do their time then get out to do it all over again.

When I first arrived in prison I was naturally on the lookout for all the horrors you hear about. Stabbings and gang rapes in particular are what I most feared. After being here for eighteen months or so I had learned the basic rules of physical survival, the nuanced etiquette necessary in relating to old timers, guards, hard-timers, fresh meat, queens, gangsters, when to be strong, when to back down, how to back down, when to joke, when not to. Physical survival is fairly easy.

The hardest, most dangerous part of being locked up is the daily threat to your mental survival, your emotional survival. At these levels, the survival rate is much, much lower. In this arena, I was being mugged every day.

When I was transferred to work in the laundry, where I met Jimmy, I thought this could be the final straw. I was already deeply depressed, silently angry. Hour by hour I was going out of my mind at the stupidity of it all. My own stupidity and the stupidity around me. I had assumed with my education and background and non-violent sheet I might be put to work in the library or the training facility or even something outside the walls. Something with a little bit of meaning.

The laundry is in the basement, of the Old House, without windows, so no natural light. It's loud, it's steamy, the machines are old, and the work is numbingly mundane. It's at the low end of the totem pole. I assumed someone didn't like me, wanted to teach me humility. It pissed me off.

14

Fresh Air

I didn't have Jimmy pegged for anything in particular. Just didn't give him much attention. Jimmy just did his job, his part, didn't say much. But after working in the laundry for a week or two, I noticed that Jimmy's sheets and cases were always neatly folded, as were the prison overalls and socks. Most guys just did quick, get-it-over fold-ups, which led to their stacks falling this way and that. Jimmy's were always exact, neatly arranged.

As might be expected, some of the convicts want their personal washing done in a particular way, and others didn't give a damn, and still others you would have thought they were dressing for a White House dinner or Meet the Press interview. Other than keeping a few cons happy, in the laundry the biggest mental challenge was how many scoops of soap to use or whether to put the dryer on extra spin cycle. Jimmy seemed to give it something more.

"You do that well," I commented one time, in passing.

He smiled, nodded his head. "On purpose," he said, almost under his breath.

I nodded back. That was a strange response, so I watched, out of the corner of my eye, over the next several days. Watching, I was surprised to realize that Jimmy did not walk stiff, or slow, like most low intelligence inmates I'd met. Rather, he was a very graceful young man, unhurried yet quietly efficient, without extra moves. Again, he was very neat, precise with the laundry.

"What do you mean on purpose?" I asked, the next time we were folding sheets next to each other. To take up a conversation where it left off days or even weeks after ending it is not uncommon in here. He studied me a long while before responding.

"I've been in and out of these joints since I was thirteen years old," he finally said, going back to the sheets. "I'm looking at another five years, at least, before I walk the streets again. They threw the little bitch at me."

'Little bitch' means extra time for repeat offenders. 'Bitch' is shorthand for "habitual."

"No one's out there waiting for me this time," he went on.

I nodded my head, but didn't understand why he was telling me this. He stared at me. So I shrugged my shoulders, as if to question.

"You got to make up a purpose," he said. "I've learned that if you don't have a purpose, your time goes twice as slow, and something starts to rot inside."

16

"So you fold laundry on purpose?" I asked, almost laughing, but I didn't. He immediately saw I been holding back a laugh, so he stared at me, studied me with cold eyes, and nodded his head a short yes. I nodded with him.

"Makes sense," I said.

"If you do it just because the Man made it your job, because he gave you your assignment, they win," he said. "If you decide to do what you do on purpose, to the very best of your ability, then you're in charge. You're free."

He put his attention back to folding sheets. So I too paid close attention to the next pair of overalls I folded. By the time I had folded three pair, for the first time in months, I felt I was breathing fresh air.

I was surprised. I looked over at Jimmy Fein. He gave me the slightest of grins, and even slighter nod. That was the beginning of my apprenticeship.

3

The Stuntman's Fortune

I was crawling home from L.A. to Daleville, Ohio with my tail between my legs. My plan had been to sneak through the back door of the movie business by jumping off burning buildings and crashing cars and motorcycles, starting off as a stunt man. And then maybe some day . . .

Instead, I first worked in a Dunkin Donuts shop and then selling stereo equipment in a strip mall on Sepulvada Boulevard. I would have preferred construction work or even lawn work, so I could enjoy the California weather, which is the other reason everybody goes out there, but I didn't speak Spanish and had no contacts.

When I first got to L.A. I slept in my car and then after getting the Dunkin' Donuts job I rented a small room in a real run-down place that used to be a motel. But compared to my car, that crowded little room felt like the Ritz. And of course I thought I was just collecting hard luck stories that I would tell later, and laugh about, after I made it big. But even that little room cost me about everything I made at Dunkin Donuts.

And then when I got the job at the stereo place they paid me okay the first three weeks, but I was supposed to be learning the business so I could work half pay, half commission. They said I'd probably earn double after that first three weeks. But I made about half. I sucked as a stereo salesman.

In the meantime, I learned that stunt men actually go to school for that stuff, and it's not a cheap school. They also have a union, and even then, like they say, it's not what you know, it's who. And I didn't know anyone except the regulars who came in for donuts and kids dreaming about a new sound system for their cars.

I'm embarrassed to admit, a lot of people in Daleville had told me I looked like a movie star, and I really enjoyed being in five different plays during high school. People told me I was a great actor, but our school was so small, if you tried out, you generally got a part.

So that Friday night in L.A., sitting in my room after getting my puny paycheck, I realized I could either put my whole check into another week's rent—which was due on Saturday—or use it to pay for gas and food to get me back to Daleville. I talked myself into Daleville by saying I'd go back, live with my folks, get a construction job, save enough to pay for stunt man school. I'd be back. I'd been in L.A. three and a half months.

It didn't take me long to pack. I didn't have that much stuff. The only thing new I had were some cool sea shells I found when I went to the beach. Once the decision was made, I couldn't stay in that room another hour. I was supposed to work on Saturday but I told myself I'd call the stereo people from the road, tell them I had an emergency back in Ohio—something to do with my mom or grandmother—who needed me back there immediately. And the motel people had a box you could drop off the key when you left for good. People were leaving all the time.

I took a last look around my dumpy little room, turned out the lights, pulled the door shut and locked it. I got in my car, dropped the key in the box by the office, and pulled onto Sepulveda, heading for the I-10.

Suddenly, and surprisingly, as I was driving away, down Sepulveda, my heart broke open and tears came to my eyes. I really had assumed that L.A. was going to be "my town"—where I made it big, made my fortune. I really did love the lights, the cars, the palm trees, the craziness. Until that moment they were *my* lights, *my* cars, *my* palm trees, my craziness, my new world. And now suddenly they weren't.

I suddenly saw myself as a stranger there, a misfit. An outsider. And I saw I always had been.

I started crying, out of loss, and regret and disappointment, and also out of relief. What I had to do now was so simple: just drive, and drive some more, drive across the mountains and then drive across the desert, drive across the plains, drive across the wheat fields, the cornfields, the bean fields, drive until I was home.

I drove most of Friday night, slept a while in my car at a rest stop alongside the road in Nevada, then drove all day Saturday, except for a few hours napping in another rest area, then again most of Saturday night, again sleeping in my car, then waking and driving some more. I never called the stereo folks. I feel bad about that.

So finally, about noon on Sunday, I pulled onto Church Street, the main drag of Daleville. I was right behind a yellow Daleville school bus, which had its yellow lights flashing. I thought it was strange for a school bus to be out on Sunday. In front of the school bus was a Daleville police car, driving slow with its bright red and blue flashers flashing. Since the school bus had its lights flashing I knew I probably shouldn't try to pass it, especially with the police car up front. So I just followed it.

As we came into town, people were lined up on both sides of the street. As the school bus passed, people cheered and waved and yelled. Many of these were people I recognized, who I had grown up with, had seen in the shops and streets. They were obviously happy to be seeing the school bus. And then when they saw me many people laughed and pointed and waved at me, as if they were happy to see me, too. I waved back.

When we came to the high school, the police car and the school bus turned off. I saw a large banner that said. "Welcome Home Ohio State Division 3 High School Champions." I found out later that the day before they had won the state championship up in Cleveland. This was their welcome-home parade.

That was fifteen years ago. I'm married now, with three children. Daleville is a good place to raise a family, a good place to be. But when watching movies with my kids, I sometimes find myself watching closely as the stunt men fall off the buildings, or go through a burning wall. I still have a secret stash of cash—that seems to dwindle—beneath my socks and underwear, sort of saving up for stunt man school. The sea shells are there too. When things settle down, maybe, some day . . .

But to tell the truth, I'm not that motivated any more. Maybe that one little parade was all I needed to be very content to be back home.

4

The Olympian's Next Quest

"I feel like I've let everybody down—not only my friends and family, but everyone, everyone..."

Lucy, back at the dormitory, back in her Olympian street clothes, her bag packed, sat in a chair on the far side of the lobby. With shoulders hunched and hands clutched between spread legs, she stared at the carpet, her head down, tears in her eyes.

"Yea right. By being one of the five fastest women in the world," said the big woman standing next to her chair. "You let down ..."

"That's it!" Lucy snapped, looking up and interrupting her best friend and trainer. "Fifth! Not even fourth, which is at least close to a medal. Fifth! Out of the running. A nobody. A non-contender."

Patty knew better than to argue with her friend, but she couldn't help it.

"Yea right. A non-contender."

These were the words that let Lucy's dam finally break: *a non-contender.* She broke into uncontrollable sobbing. Images rose up in her mind of hour after hour at the track, of working through all the pains, in her legs, her shoulders, her back, the constant knot in her stomach, and the cost! Thinking of the cost, she sobbed even more. Her parents had paid for so many trips, so many hotels, for trainers and special camps. They'd sold their motor home and boat, insisting, "Those things weren't as much fun as watching you run." She now knew different.

They had sacrificed so much, all for her, all for this one day. Now they had nothing to show for it.

Patty sat down in the chair next to Lucy, put her arm around her, rubbing her shoulder, letting her cry. The other athletes in the lobby gave nervous glances in their direction then hurried past. They all knew too well these moments.

"You're an Olympian," Patty whispered, patting her back. "Just being on the team—being here, able to compete with the world's best, is an amazing accomplishment."

"I know, I know," Lucy said, nodding her head, slowly catching her breath. An image came of the trophy shelf in her parents' dining room. And then she cried some more. They'd be waiting, with all the other parents and friends, at the downtown hotel. Organized sight-seeing was still ahead. She couldn't bear the thought. She wanted to crawl into a bed, far from anybody she knew, curl up, hide beneath covers.

"I've let everybody down," she said again. Patty was tempted to say something about "next time," but she and Lucy both knew there would be no "next time." Lucy had narrowly missed making the team four years previously. At that time, everyone assured her she had not yet come into her full power, her full strength. They were right. In these last years she had steadily grown better, faster, more confident, more refined, more consistent. She truly was at her peak. And she had run her fastest race ever, against the best in the world, and had come in fifth, less than one full second behind the first four.

But still, fifth.

Patty, as trainer, was ready to be done with this whole show. It had been a great ride. A great trip. Her own personal coaching and training career was as strong as ever. This trip to the Olympics would only enhance it, regardless of Lucy's personal disappointment. But now, candidly, she was ready for some sight-seeing, good food, good wine, the company of ordinary, unexceptional, quick-to-laughter people.

Patty looked across the lobby and saw the bus pull up outside that would take them into the city, to the hotel where Lucy's parents were waiting, where they would stay for the remainder of their time here.

"Okay sister," Patty said, patting Lucy on the shoulder. "Our ride's here."

Lucy looked up at Patty. "Did I let you down?" she asked. "Are you really disappointed in me?"

Patty looked her in the eyes a long moment, not saying anything. Lucy waited for her response. Finally, Patty spoke.

"Yea, you slacker. What the hell were you doing out there? Looked like you were picking daisies, just skipping and humming to yourself. You forget where you were, the World Olympics?"

Lucy cracked, broke into a small smile. She stood, picked up her bag. "The World Olympics?" she said. "the one I'd been training for? Now you tell me. What type of third rate—no fifth rate-- trainer are you?"

Patty nodded her head, smiled, picked up her own bags. "Hell with 'em," she said. "Let's go find us some donuts."

5

The Prophet's Mercy

When the bus pulled to the curb in the busy street, Iyad reached for the handle on the outside door, stepped up, whispering to himself. "God is One. God is all. There is only one God. *Allah Ackbar*." His eyelids were fluttering. He held his other hand and arm straight down.

"*Suicider! Suicider!*" someone on the bus shouted. The heavy steel door immediately started to close.

"*Allah Akbar*," Iyad said one last time as he raised his arm, which pulled the cord attached to the explosives around his waist.

The blast racked the bus, blew off its doors, turned it into a fireball. Windows shattered up and down the blocks. Traffic stopped. Sirens wailed. People were screaming and crying.

"God is all. God is one. There is only one God," Iyad kept repeating.

"Peace and blessing be upon the Prophet and his messengers," he heard a voice say. "You are now counted amongst his favored martyrs."

Iyad opened his eyes and saw, fleetingly, the oily grin and burning eyes of Mustafeed, his handler.

"My baby! My baby!" He heard a woman's voice wail. Iyad could see the burning bus below him, the people running, the traffic snarled. He could hear the sirens.

"Now my parents will be cared for, and I will go to Paradise," he remembered. He thought of beautiful girls and flowing streams and flower gardens. He closed his eyes and was no longer present.

The soft cooing of pigeons brought him awake again. He didn't know how long he had been asleep—or away—or where he had gone. And he didn't know where he was, or how he was. Again, the cooing of pigeons.

Iyad suddenly saw black pupils, outlined in red, a gray feathered head, a gray beak with white spot, just inches away. Iyad jerked back. He saw two other pigeons on the ledge, which was stained with their droppings. "God is all. God is one." Iyad said out of long habit.

"We did not send you but as a Mercy to all the worlds," a quiet voice responded. Iyad could not tell whether it was a man's or woman's voice, but it was clear and simple and full of truth. He had heard this phrase a thousand times since he was a child, but only now did the words reveal their meaning.

Iyad realized he was on the ledge of the building overlooking the square. Somehow he was aware that the explosion—his explosion—had startled the pigeons into flight and that they were just now returning to their roost. He was awed, and somewhat stunned that his actions had had such a small, temporary influence on these birds.

Again, he heard the voice. "The Prophet was sent as a mercy to all the worlds."

And now Iyad's eyes, from his perch at the top of the building, found the scene below. From the way they were dressed, he recognized a Muslim man kneeling beside an old Jewish woman sprawled in the street. The man was stroking her hair. Other people were sitting on the curbs, or standing or also lying in the streets. Jews, Christians and Muslims were all working frantically to help each other recover from the blast, holding cloths against their wounds, bringing water, clearing debris.

"The Prophet was sent with a sword," he heard—or was he simply remembering—Mustafeed's voice. The pigeons briefly fluttered up and settled again. For a moment, a long moment, Iyad could not remember how the Prophet's sword brings mercy, though Mustafeed had schooled them long and hard about the necessity of this jihad.

"My mercy embraces all things," the other voice said, repeating words from the Koran. And in that moment Iyad saw how everything—everything—all the buildings, all the people, the trees and flowers, even the shattered glass on the pavement, but especially the people—everywhere he looked all he could see was God's mercy. Even the pools of blood on the street were radiant with life, with mercy, with eternal presence.

And suddenly the Prophet was in front of him. He knew it was the Prophet. His eyes were full of mercy. He was radiant with wisdom and power. The sky opened around the Prophet and Iyad could see to the edge of the universe how God's mercy was the rule.

And then the vision faded. Iyad was again back on the ledge with the pigeons, watching the scene below. He wished he could help. He wanted to bring mercy, show mercy.

Iyad stayed on the ledge, watching, wishing, hoping, for many earth years, though from his perspective it felt like an eternity. Finally, finally, after many decades, he felt a true glimmer of mercy rise up in his heart for that foolish boy who had caused such suffering, and those who had so misled him.

The pigeons still cooed.

6

The Bishop's Inquiry

In a classic gesture of puzzlement, Bishop Andrew Wozcoski studied the Excel spreadsheet appearing on his computer screen while simultaneously stroking his well-shaven chin, as if he had a beard there. Something strange, but good, was going on out at Saint Catherine's.

The Bishop had appointed that plucky little priest, Father William Snopes ("Father Billy," his parishioners called him) to the failing Parish hoping to bring new life to a slowly ebbing suburban congregation. Of course, almost all of the Bishop's churches were slowly ebbing, but the suburb itself, Westchester, was growing steadily, and the church should not have been losing so many members. The Bishop had replaced the long-standing Father Bernard (never known as "Father Bernie") who had been at Saint Catherine's for over twenty-two years. His decision to replace Father Bernard with Father Billy had caused an uproar in the church, with much resistance from the old stalwarts, and deeply felt, harshly worded pleas for mercy and reconsideration.

The replacement had worked. After an initial drop in membership—which had been expected, accounting for the loss of parishioners disgruntled with the Bishop's decision—membership had begun to slowly but steadily recover, and then surpass previous membership. That had been four and half years ago. The Bishop had been pleased with the results. But something dramatic and surprising had happened six months previously. Both membership and per capita average monthly donations increased so dramatically that a red flag was flapping as the Bishop studied his charts.

Leaning back in his chair, studying the spread sheet, stroking his chin, his eyebrows furled, the Bishop made another decision. He sat forward in his chair and reached for the phone.

"So what's up?" Virginia asked when Tom, her husband came back inside with the phone. She was sitting at the kitchen table with a cup of coffee. When the phone first rang, Virginia answered. It was the Bishop. After exchanging the usual pleasantries—she knew the Bishop well—he asked to speak with Tom.

"He wants us to start attending St. Catherine's again. Find out what's going on. Something good this time."

Virginia was a bit disappointed that the Bishop hadn't talked to her about it, but man-talk, men making manly decisions, was part of the tradition. Tom and

Virginia had conducted quiet investigations like this for the Bishop when he wanted a parishioner's view of what was going on inside the church. Five years earlier they had attended St. Catherine's—a thirty minute drive across town – to get an insider's view of Father Bernard's approach. After attending for several months, volunteering on committees and work duties, they had made their report to the Bishop. It had not been their first foray into acting as the "Bishop's eyes." Nor the last. For Virginia, such clandestine activities took much of the boredom out of Tom's lifelong commitment to Catholicism. Virginia had been brought up as a Methodist, had converted when they were married, but was not as fervent as Tom. For instance, she was insistent that their two children—Sadie, now nine, and Daniel, sixteen—were children enough . She used birth control.

Four years ago, Father Bernard's transfer was a perfect excuse to ease out of their St Catherine's membership, and return to their original parish.

"He's funny," Virginia said to Tom, on their way back to the car, coming out of St. Catherine's the next Sunday. "That's refreshing.

"Yea, I liked him," Tom agreed. "Seems like a very up-beat guy. And the people seem to enjoy him a lot. There's a good feeling in this church."

As was their custom, Tom and Virginia slowly integrated themselves over the next six weeks into the church community. Father Billy himself welcomed them, encouraged them, was surprised yet delighted they were making the trip from across the city to attend St. Catherine's. And the congregation welcomed new helping hands on various committees.

"Forgive me Father, for I have sinned," Virginia whispered in the confessional at St. Catherine's one Thursday afternoon. This was her first confession at St. Catherine's. According to tradition, before taking Holy Communion on Sunday one should make confession at least once during the week, and if at all possible to do so in a confessional booth. Both she and Tom had found it easier to go to confession at their old, regular church—St. Bart's—Saint Bartholomew—since it was so much closer. They'd told Father Billy this is what they were doing, since they did take communion at St. Catherine's on Sunday. He said that was perfectly fine, perfectly appropriate. He was very easy-going.

Since she was brought up Methodist, Virginia had always been secretly a bit skeptical about the practice, but went along with Tom's belief that it was necessary and good for the soul to tell another living human being about one's failings. Virginia did generally feel a bit better after confession, but sometimes secretly wished she had more serious sins to confess.

That Thursday, Virginia confessed her usual sins of coveting her neighbor's possessions and bearing ill will against her neighbor and being prideful and being forgetful, or at least lax in her daily devotions.

Father Billy—she knew it was Father Billy though it's supposed to be anonymous--- said all the things a priest is supposed to say and gave her penance.

"Is that all, child?" Father asked at the end.

"Yes, thank you Father."

"Before you go, let me suggest you might also confess—or just share— a few of your joys, your triumphs, what you are perhaps privately proud about but hesitate, out of humility and social grace, to speak about in ordinary life."

"What?" Virginia asked.

"It's a little something we added to confession six months or so ago, " Father Billy said. "It seems to work. So what are you happy about, Virginia?" Using her name was also not the custom in these circumstances. "What made you laugh this week? What made you proud of yourself or your husband or your kids? What are you glad about that you did or thought or felt?"

Virginia laughed. "Now this is the type of confession I can get into," she said.

Father Billy laughed, too. "Yes. All aspects of Church life should be something you enjoy, and look forward to. If you don't enjoy your activities, don't do them."

"I confess I don't really enjoy confessing my sins," Virginia said.

"A lot of people feel that way. Most who come here now skip that part," Father Billy said. "Unless they have something really troubling them, weighing on them. If it's not a weight on your heart, you are free to skip right to confessing your joys, your triumphs, your secret victories and delights that you're not able to tell elsewhere. Even something so simple as how good you look with your new hair style."

Virginia laughed again. She did have a new hair style and she did feel it made her look quite a bit younger. She was tickled, and impressed, that Father Billy noticed.

"Thank you, Father."

The Bishop's Inquiry

"What else are you happy about? " he asked.

That evening, Virginia decided not to tell Tom about her experience in the Confessional. Not yet. Let him find out, if he ever decided to go across town.

And as far as her report to the Bishop— she'd let him go to the confessional, too. Let him find out for himself what was happening at St. Catherine's. As far as Virginia was concerned, what happens in the confessional booth stays in the confessional booth. Some things in life are more real, more important, more *interesting* than the bishop's inquiry.

7.

How Civilization Grows

Because of the chill, this morning Harry Winston was again grateful the bus stop was in front of his house. He could wait on his own glassed-in front porch, out of the icy wind, almost until the bus arrived before slowly making his way down the granite steps to catch the 7:42 number 16 to downtown.

He had lived in this house for forty years—thirty-three with Ellen, until she'd passed. When they'd bought the house Barton Avenue had been an auxiliary street, busy during rush hours but otherwise not bad. Had it been on a side street, the large two story brick house would have been out of their price range. In the years since then Barton Avenue had become a major thoroughfare, busy day and night. The city had added a bus line sixteen years ago, with a bus stop smack in front of their house, since they lived on the corner.

This morning, Harry Winston was in the middle of his third month of self-directed mind training. He wanted to train himself to stay focused no matter what else was happening around him so as he stepped on to the bus he was holding a clip board with a thin sheet of twenty-five three-digit math problems.

The 7:42a.m. Bus Number 16 was double extended and standing room only. That's why Harry had chosen it for his mind training. Quite often someone would stand and offer him a seat, but just as often he would decline. "Thank you, but I prefer to stand. It's good practice for my balance," he'd say.

Harry kept his sheet of math problems on a clip board so he could write down the answers. He'd look at the problem, say 327 plus 269, and then add it in his head, write down the answer. His challenge to himself was to complete twenty-five problems in the twenty-eight minutes it took the bus to reach civic center.

When he first started his training he took a mid-morning or mid-afternoon bus, where there was always a place to sit. He had successfully completed all the problems with almost 100% accuracy. Rather than add more problems, which he always wrote out on notebook paper the night before, he decided he needed more distractions. Thus, the change to the rush hour 7:42. He most often did get a seat in the last ten to fifteen minutes, as the bus cleared out. He was much quicker, more efficient when he was sitting down.

"Hey pops, what you doing there every day?" a young black man asked this morning. The young man was standing near where Harry was standing with his arm crooked lightly to a pole. "Figuring out race horses? Or stock market? I seen you do it every day."

Harry looked up and smiled. "Just practicing my numbers," he said. "Keeping my old brain waters flowing." Harry looked back down at his clipboard.

The young man stared at him. "Practicing your numbers?" he asked, in disbelief. Harry smiled, nodded, but kept his eyes on the problem he was working on. Three hundred and eighty-six minus two hundred and fourteen. Harry had learned to respond politely but reservedly to commuters who wanted to talk. Generally, when he went back to his clipboard, they would turn their attention elsewhere.

"You still in school or something, still at your age?" the young man asked, not threatening, but as if he really wanted to know.

Harry looked up, smiled again. "No. Well, my own school. I'm teaching myself." He nodded, then looked back down at his numbers.

"Teaching yourself numbers?"

The young man really was insistent, and curious. Harry looked at him a long moment, trying to decide how to respond.

"No, not numbers, really. Concentration. I'm teaching myself concentration."

"Does it work?" the young man asked.

Just then the bus stopped, doors opened near them, people got on and off, interrupting their talk. "One hundred and seventy-two," Harry thought. He let go of the pole, balanced and wrote it down on his paper. As the doors closed and the bus accelerated, Harry again held on to the pole. He smiled at the young man.

"Yes, it works," he said.

"So you teach yourself concentration?"

Again Harry just smiled and nodded and looked back at the next problem. Nine hundred and seventy two minus three hundred and eighty-four.

"You do this every day. I been watching you," the young man said again.

Harry looked up. Nodded his head. "I do."

"On purpose? Just to train yourself concentration?" Again, Harry just smiled, nodded his head.

"Nobody makes you?"

Harry shook his head.

"And you don't use these numbers to play the ponies, or stock market?"

"Nope, just for fun," Harry said, looking up at the young man to actually be present with him for a moment.

"I never knew people could do that," the young man said, shaking his head. "I mean, learn stuff, learn concentration, just for fun."

The young man grew quiet, watched Harry. "Will you teach me?" he asked.

Harry was surprised. He looked up. "Concentration? You want to learn concentration?"

"Yea, that would be okay. But I want to learn how to learn something just for fun. All on my own. I didn't know you could that."

The two men stared at each other for a long moment.

"I take this bus every day. And I been watching you. Will you teach me how to learn just for fun?"

Harry grinned big. "I suppose I could do that," he said. "Might be fun."

"This is my stop," the young man said, as the bus pulled over at Boyleston Street. "I see you tomorrow."

Harry nodded his head, watching the young man skip down the steps and onto the street. As the bus pulled away, Harry turned to watch the young man through the window. The young man waved. Harry waved back. Further down the block, Harry took a seat and put his clip board aside.

"How can I teach someone how to learn just for fun?" he wondered. It was a problem worth his concentration.

8

Slick Vic's Next Work

After the ship went down Slick Vic found himself bobbing in the water, clinging to the wooden rudder which was still attached to a piece of the wooden aft beam. After coughing out sea water and trying to catch his breath, Slick Vic held to the rudder while he scanned the choppy sea around him.

He'd been aloft in the crow's nest when the ship exploded. Most of the rest of the crew were below decks, celebrating the capture of a Portuguese frigate, dividing the spoils. Second Mate O'Reilly was at the wheel, directly above the cache of black powder. Slick Vic had been sent to the crow's nest, with much laughter and ridicule from the rest of the crew.

"You're too old and grumpy to enjoy such a party," the captain had said, though it was the captain who would make sure Vic would receive his fair share of the spoils. In truth, the captain was right. Vic preferred the crow's nest, the wind and the view and the muffled voices below, though it took him longer than any of his mates to climb his way to the roost.

The wanted posters with a sketch of his face from twenty years ago gave his name as Victor Conner Dinsmore, aka Slick Vick. He had been "Slick

Vic," or simply Vic, for over fifty years, since he was a young boy on the docks in Bristol.

When the ship exploded, he immediately assumed some drunken pipe smoker had accidentally stumbled into the store of black powder with a lit pipe. Vic saw second mate O'Reilly rise into the air, engulfed in a ball of flames, just as he himself went down with the tilting and splintering mast.

Now bobbing, holding on to the wooden rudder, Vic was surrounded with floating shreds of wood, and pieces of clothes and other detritus of what for too many years to count had been his only home. Vic drew a picture in his mind of his location and options: he was at least a hundred miles off the shores of Tripoli. After the capture of the Portuguese frigate they had intentionally steered thirty leagues away from the main shipping lines between Liverpool and Johannesburg, hoping to avoid capture by those who had put a reward on the capture of this Jolly Roger sloop.

So the chances of another ship coming by were slim. And even if it should happen, once they discovered his work, his tattoos would give him away. If he was not immediately put into chains, Slick Vic would probably be hung from the mast or be made to walk the plank with weights attached to his legs.

"So this is how it ends," Vic whispered out loud, clinging to his rudder. His words were immediately absorbed and made mute by the wide ocean and empty sky.

"Hello, hello, hello," he shouted, hoping someone, anyone, had also survived the blast. And again his words were swallowed by the sea, sucked dry into the sky.

Images from the arc of his life began appearing in rapid succession. Stealing bits of food with his brothers on the docks of Bristol. The years in the army, at war. The bloodshed, the stupidity, the widows. The ladies he'd known in the various ports. The dead-end years on the Jolly Roger, which he knew all along would lead to nothing, would lead to this, or worse.

Vic assumed this circumstance was his last, his mind and heart were hopeless. This truly was the end. Yet he knew himself well-enough to recognize that if he should just give up, let go, he'd soon swim back up, grab on again, even here. Even now, the life in him would not give up.

"So this is how it ends," he said and again, said it out loud. Somehow, now, after the initial panic, after the many images of his past, somehow now it seemed both strange and funny and quite appropriate, even beautiful that it should all end this way, alone in the sea. He felt how lonely he had been all his life. A light breeze came across the water, carrying the scent of salt and rain. And then it began to rain, soft, gentle, nourishing drops.

Slick Vic smiled, and closed his eyes and lifted his face into the rain. Once again, out loud, he said, "This is how Slick Vic dies." He breathed in deep, welcoming all the sensations, the ocean that gently moved his legs, the ache in his arms as he clung to the shipless rudder, the last hint of the taste of the dried fish and figs he'd eaten for lunch.

This, *this* was how it ends. Slick Vick was willing, he was ready. It had all been worth it, even the loneliness, just for this last hint of the taste of dried fish and figs, this taste of life. He opened his eyes.

"What?"

When at the top of the wave, he could see there in the far, far distance, the hint of a palm tree above the sea. It must be an island. His heart fluttered. This might not be the end after all. Slick Vick started kicking, guiding his rudder that way.

9

THE CLOSING

The snow was beginning to fall from a grey late afternoon sky when Larry stashed his large level and Sawz-All into the tool box on the back of his truck. These were the last of his tools. He was done. They were done. He locked the box.

Tomorrow the relators would close on this monstrosity of a house, what he and the rest of the crew referred to as the Gardner Place. It was on Gardner Avenue. He needn't be at the closing, of course. He was the help.

He'd been hired six months earlier as both finish carpenter and crew boss by his cousin Danny. Larry knew he should take one more empty-handed trip through the place—just to make sure he hadn't left anything behind, and to take a last look at his and the crew's work on this 7500 square foot custom McMansion overlooking a lake and the city. Some senior vice-president for Boxwin Grain and Trading company would now have his new primary residence, to compliment his smaller "fun" vacation houses in Aspen and Naples.

Knowing he should go back and check things out one last time, Larry suddenly felt drained, and tired of the whole thing. He was proud and confident of his work. After forty-two years in the trade, you develop some skills, some tricks, some knacks. You could build things that would last a long time, and fit well and look nice in their place. He'd done a good job. But suddenly he was drained. He leaned his forearms on the bed of his truck. He hung his head.

"Yo, Larry, yokay?" Pete Winslow, the tile man, called from the porch. Larry lifted his head, nodded yes, waved, then let his head fall again.

Maybe it was this last rush to get everything done before closing. They'd been putting in 12 and 14 hour days. And now that it was done, he realized how tired, how drained he was. In fact, he needed to just sit down here for minute, before making that last walk through the house. He held to the truck bed, turned and let himself ease down. He sat on the ground, leaning against the rear tire. He gently let his head fall back against the fender, and closed his eyes.

As he often did, Larry thought how much he missed Willette, his wife of thirty-two years, passed last year from her life-long struggle with MS. And he thought of his own nine hundred and eight square foot home that he built himself, mortgage free. He thought about the Mortenson place, that they were supposed to start next week.

He'd been thinking he'd like to maybe take some time off between houses. Maybe go fishing. Maybe just sit on his porch.

"Yokay, Larry?" he heard his cousin asking, bending over him. Larry briefly opened his eyes, closed them, nodded his head.

"Just tired, need a little rest," were his last words before closing down for good.

10

Not Always This Friendly

After serving eighteen years, seven months and twenty-one days (but who's counting?) in the Illinois state prison at Joliet— armed robbery resulting in injury or death by a repeat offender—I had to come up with a plan for what I was going to do when I was released. In fact, no plan, no release. I'd had eighteen years, seven months and twenty-one days to think about it, but I was still a little unclear.

I'd grown up on Chicago's south side, a free-wheeling, happy-go-lucky kid who hung out with other free-wheeling, happy-go-lucky kids, without much supervision, such that we ended up not so happy, not so lucky and no longer either free or wheeling, and with 24-7 supervision. But that's another story.

My plan after my release—or at least what I told the Parole Board—was to go live and work in the boondocks of Nebraska on my grandparents' farm with my two cousins, Jesse and Bubba. Actually, the boondocks was the nearest town— Lewellyn, population two hundred and forty-eight. Except, as my cousin Bubba said, laughing, all the Nelsons had packed up and left so the population was actually two hundred and thirty four.

So my grandparents' farm was in the boondocks of the boondocks—six miles outside of Lewellyn. My parole officer would be in Kearny— one hundred and eighty miles to the east, which was fine with me. The further away, the better.

Which is exactly how the people in Illinois felt about me. So it was sort of a win-win deal.

We used to drive to Nebraska when I was a kid and my folks were still together. My dad had grown up on the farm, but then he'd gone in the army, so that he could become a man and learn some discipline, or at least that was the plan. The army didn't make him a man so much as it made him a bully, and a brute. The discipline he learned was Jack Daniels and coke, starting as a mid-morning hair of the dog. But that's another story.

I used to play in Grandpa's barn with Bubba and Jesse when we would visit. Although they were a few years older than me, they were about the same age as each other—six months apart— and they were cousins who lived down the road from each other. Aunt Alice and Uncle Roy were Bubba's folks. Aunt Opel and Uncle Charlie were Jesse's folks. Uncle Charlie helped Grandpa on the farm and Uncle Roy had a farm just down the road from Grandpa's.

By the time I got out of prison Bubba and Jesse were working together and owned several farms and feed lots around Lewellyn. "Sure, we can always use more help," Jesse had told me on one of the calls I'd made from Joliet. "You won't get rich, but you'll get by. And it's a good life. So we'd be honored to be your sponsors, cuz. Besides, you're family. Anything we can do . . ."

Naturally, I was a bit worried, in fact quite doubtful that I could fit into such a life, after the one I'd lived. So I'd made some back up plans, with a couple of old hands in Denver, just in case. I didn't find it necessary to mention these back-up plans to my parole officer. Or to Bubba or Jesse.

I got off the bus in Oshkosh, which was the nearest town with bus service. I had ridden twelve hours from Chicago, with transfers in Moline and Lincoln. Both Jesse and Bubba were waiting for me, standing just outside the bus door. Both of them broke into huge grins when they saw me come down the bus steps. Although it had been more than thirty years since we'd last seen each other, I recognized them immediately., Mostly by their smiles. I waved tentatively.

Bubba had grown into a typical Nebraska farmer, big, beefy, in overalls and a baseball cap. Jesse looked like a typical Nebraska cowboy, lean as a fence post, white cowboy hat and cowboy shirt and blue jeans.

"Hello guys" I said. "Thanks for meeting me. Thanks for being here."

"The prodigal son," Bubba laughed, opening his arms wide, as if ready for a hug. "Home from the wars. Let us slay the fatted calf." And with that he stepped forward and embraced me, pulled me tight against his overalls.

Bubba's a good five inches taller and a hundred pounds heavier than me. He kissed me on top of the head and just kept hugging and hugging.

Suddenly, and unexpectedly, tears came to my eyes. Bubba finally let me go, grabbed me by the shoulders, held me at arm's length. "What a sight for sore eyes," he said. I nodded.

Then Jesse stepped forward. He was not five inches taller, but three or four inches taller than me. Without saying anything, he put me in a head lock and gave me a Dutch rub. "Hello, little cuz," he said. "Welcome home." Then he, too, lifted my head and gave the top of it a kiss.

I had been thinking I'd stay a day or two and then disappear, hitchhike on to Denver, following my back-up plan where an old cell mate had a potential pay-day waiting. But now, maybe, just maybe, I'd stick around here a little longer. See what these guys, my flesh and blood cousins, were really up to. See what they were really like. Surely, they were not always this friendly.

Without thinking, I let out a deep breath, and felt my shoulders relax as they hadn't relaxed in a long, long time. Tears came back to my eyes.

"Okay cowboy," Bubba said, putting his fleshy palm around my shoulder as Jesse took my bag from me. "Let's go on home."

11

Famous Frank's Dilemma

Famous Frank Angosotti—no longer the name on his driver's license —sat on a public bench next to the bike path that ran alongside the river, slowly eating his lunch—ham and cheese on pastrami; a boiled egg, potato chips, celery sticks. He'd made and packed the sack lunch himself, of course. There was no one else in his life to do it. He was three blocks from the Johnson Printing and Publishing Plant, where he now worked.

Several years earlier, Famous Frank had turned state's evidence—it was the only way to avoid ten to fifteen in Altoona on racketeering charges. After testifying, he then went into the Federal Witness Protection program.

Here now, eating his lunch, it slowly dawned on Frank that the real challenge on this new road he was traveling was not staying hidden, staying anonymous, staying away from those who would pay money to see him dead. Staying hidden was fairly easy. The Feds did a good job of creating not just a fake history for his new name, but also references from past employers, credit scores, a new social security number of course, lasik surgery so he no longer wore glasses, even a little plastic surgery to change the shape of his nose.

And they found him steady employment. As a teenager Frank had worked in his Uncle Tony's print shop—which did most of its business at night and off the books for a clientele who needed official papers, like birth and death certificates, immigration authentication or international trade documents and warehouse receipts. So working for a printing company was work Frank knew how to do.

Staying hidden, staying anonymous was actually the easiest part of this new life. The real challenge, he now realized, while nibbling on his sandwich was actually *being* anonymous, being nobody. Back in the day, Famous Frank had openly enjoyed being called Famous Frank. In fact, many of his closest friends simply called him "Fame." He liked that, too. And he had dressed the part, from tuxes and pin-striped suits to pirate shirts. He would regularly show up to parties, to restaurants and recitals in a stretch limo.

"It's all bullshit. All an act," he would joke with his friends, so that they knew he wasn't getting too big of a head. "But it's fun bullshit. Exciting bullshit. I have to live up to the name."

Here in this new town, with his new name and new history, a few new friends and new job, what he missed most was being famous. Actually, he knew he hadn't been that famous. Not real famous, like famous people, movie stars and politicians, business billionaires.

But he enjoyed his neighborhood fame, his borough fame, even a little Big Apple fame. Even more, he enjoyed plotting and conniving and strategizing every day on what he could do to become a bit more famous in his little world.

Of course, that all blew up in his face when the whole organization had the rug pulled out from under it. Having done the printing plant stint, and then working his way up from there, he had more scoop on more people than even he had realized. Being still fairly young—just turned forty-five—and his own crimes, at least as far as the Feds knew, not so egregious that cutting this deal would be a gross injustice to justice itself—Frank made the front pages of the *Times* every day for a week as he testified against his former friends and associates, even his Uncle Tony, who fortunately had already retired and gone back to Sicily. This was not the type of fame—the "good guy, happy friend, larger than life" type of fame—that Frankie had always sought. This front-page newspaper fame was fame of a completely different sort, and Frank had hated it.

In this new town, no one knew him, no one recognized him, and for his own safety from here on out he had to make this ordinary anonymity his daily standard operating procedure. That being the case, Frank was at a loss of what to do with his life, what to do with his mind.

Frank was content with the salary he earned at Johnsons. He had directly experienced how making lots of money did not lead to experiencing lots of happiness. He was over that. He was earning enough money to lead a decent life. Making more money was not a problem, nor was it an interesting challenge.

Salting his boiled egg, Frank wondered what ordinary people thought about, what they did, if they weren't always trying to get rich or be famous?

Chewing slowly on the egg, a kingfisher flew into the tree down the path. The blue-capped, blue-winged plumage caught Frank's eye. Frank didn't know it was a kingfisher. Frank knew a robin when he saw one, and a crow. Or a sparrow. He didn't know what kind of bird this blue-capped guy was.

The kingfisher let out its three-toned warble, not jut once, but again and again.

"Trying to get some attention, there, buster?" Frank asked out loud, as he wrapped up his lunch, put it back in the bag. "I guess that's natural."

Frank still had a little time, 15 minutes or so before he had to be back to work. He thought he might take a short walk. The blue plumed kingfisher flew to a distant tree as Frank walked by. Maybe tonight, on his way home, he'd buy a bird book, see if he could find the name of this spiffy-dressed bird.

12

WAR, AGAIN

(After Luigi Pirandello's "War")

"That's it, cock suckers," Robert Wilson O'Reilly the 2nd said to the television. "You never learn. You never fuckin' learn. So this is finally fucking it! It's time you learned." He stood from his overstuffed chair, then grabbed the arm a minute, almost falling. He was a bit wobbly from the Jack and Coors. Standing straight again, chin in, he stumbled off to find his car keys. He was heading for the Dairy Queen. He'd teach the cock sucks.

He reached into the closet and pulled out his Glock 19 9mm Compact Semi-Automatic Pistol. He always kept it fully loaded.

The television had announced that the President had ordered use of B1 Bombers and F-16 Fighter Jets for renewed bombing of what the President called "terrorist strongholds." Robert O'Reilly knew what terrorist strongholds meant.

"I *ate* your fucking terrorist strongholds," he said to the television, as he put his arm through his old army p-jacket. "Quang Tri Province, 1971. First Army." He belched. "Fucking Quang Tri. Fucking army." Tears came to his eyes. To catch his breath, he sat heavily for a moment on the bench he kept next to his front door. He rested the pistol beside him. "Eleven fucking villages. That's what was left. Three thousand fucking villages in Quang Tri, we left eleven. Eleven tiny little mother fucking villages. The rest of the mother fuckers, twenty-nine hundred villages, bombed flat. Terrorist strongholds. We flattened that fucking Terrorist Quang Tri Stronghold... The Massacre of Quang Tri, they called it. I saw it. My own fucking eyes." He rubbed his nose on his sleeve, grabbed the pistol, stood up and walked outside, leaving the door open.

"Can't bomb the fuckers away, man," Robert O'Reilly muttered to himself as he approached his Plymouth Reliant, sitting under the carport. "Not from thirty thousand feet, or twenty thousand feet or ten thousand feet or five hundred feet or fifty feet..." He opened the driver's side door. "You can't bomb the fuckers away. And when you try.... When you try... You get The Massacre of fucking Quang Tri Province."

He slid heavily into the old torn seat of the Plymouth. Put the pistol on the seat next to him. His habit was to back the Plymouth in so it was heading toward the street when he was ready. Good call on his part this time. He was not sure he could back out this morning. He fumbled the key into the ignition and turned it on.

He put the car into gear and slowly moved out from under the carport. "Just 'cause some stupid teenage gook next door is hiding in his pitiful little hut holding his stupid little Russian rifle, you massacre the whole fuckin village. And every surrounding village. Kids and grandmas can't help what the stupid shit next door is doing. They don't know the stupid little shit thinks he's protecting his fucking pitiful little village. Fuck."

Robert O'Reilly made it out of his driveway and turned up the street. He continued his drunken monolog. "What the stupid little fucker hiding with his little pee shooter is actually doing (*acshually*) —though he doesn't know it—he's calling in all the fucking bombers from hell. Just because he's hiding in his hut, the whole fucking village gets flamed, flattened. Jagged bones, sticking out of the mud. Jesus. Nobody ever learns..."

Feeling a bit dizzy, O'Reilly pulled over to the side of the street, still there in the trailer park. He leaned his head on the steering wheel, his foot on the brake, though leaving it in gear. After a moment, he sat back up, and pulled into the street again. "Besides," he said, belching again, "Who knows who the fuck lives next door these days?"

Robert O'Reiily had no heart for the terrorists. Course not, mother fucks. "So what the fuck's the difference," he muttered as the Plymouth made its way slowly out of the trailer park and onto Wilson Parkway, "between the fucking random acts of violence done by the mother fucking terrorists who kill your innocent civilians ...." he belched, wishing he'd remembered to bring a little something to drink, "....and the mother fucking President's random act of violence, from 10,000 feet? Killing your innocent civilians. Just what the fuck's the difference?"

He stopped at the four way stop sign on Oakwood Street. A new model beige Lincoln Navigator driven by a short, fat balding man in a blue leisure-suite started to slowly cross the intersection. "That's it, you air-bombing mother-fuck," O'Reilly said, taking his foot off the brake. "I'm not waiting for the Dairy Queen." He decided to ram this Republican Lincoln-driving mother-fuck, right here, right now. Then the thought crossed his mind that he just carried liability on this old Buick, and okay, he was a little late with his payment. They might argue. He slowly put his foot back on the brake. Then his head on the steering wheel.

"Bobby, Bobby, Bobby," he cried. It was in this moment, at the four way stop, with the beige Lincoln crossing safely in front of him, that for the first time in five and half years he let himself cry about the death of Marine Corporal Robert Wilson O'Reilly the third,

Seventh Cavalry Division, Second Battalion, in the Battle of Fallujah, the flattening of Fallujuah, the Massacre of Fallujah. The terrorist stronghold.

"My Bobby, my poor little Bobby."

Robert sobbed, his chest heaving, his head on the wheel, so long and so hard that a man behind him at the stop finally got out of his car and came up and knocked on his window.

"Hey, you okay mister?"

Robert Wilson O'Reilly the Second was named after Robert Wilson O'Reilly the first, who died in the Malmedy Massacre, Battle of the Bulge, December 17th 1944 when Robert was two. Robert the second looked at the stranger and shook his head, no, no, he was not okay. This shit was not okay.

"Bobby," he cried again, finally, looking face to face at this stranger.

13

Mandatory Poetry

"What the hell good is making rhymes going to do?"

"Nothing. Just like doing it."

"You should write dirty stuff. About titties and poon tang. That'd at least be interesting."

Franklin didn't know what to say to this last remark by the big kid rummaging through his school bag. The big kid was sitting on the steps of St. Joseph's church, Franklin's school bag in front of him.

"This is piss poor boring stuff," the big kid said.

"I told you I didn't have anything."

"And I was supposed to believe you? Like you'd tell me you had a wad of fifty dollar bills and dirty pictures and candy bars stuffed inside?"

Franklin shrugged his shoulders.

"Every kid tells me they got nothing. But I always find something. Except you. You got nothing."

"I told you," Franklin said again, quietly.

"So why'd you write rhyme stuff like this?" the boy asked, pointing to the small, hard-bound blue notebook. The notebook, etched with red designs, had been a gift from his sister. Three quarters of the pages were still blank.

"Did your teacher make you?" the boy asked.

"No."

"Then why'd you make them?"

"I just like to."

"Okay, make up a rhyme, right now," the boy said, jutting his chin at Franklin.

"I can't. That's not how it works."

"Why? How does it work?"

"I have to think about it. Or it just has to come to me."

"Okay, well think about it. Right now. Make up a rhyme."

Franklin looked at the ground and shook his head.

"What if I told you I'd punch you in the nose if you didn't make up a rhyme."

Franklin looked up. "If you punch me in the nose, I'd stomp on your toes."

"Hey," the big kid laughed, his eyes lighting up. "You did it. You said a rhyme."

"I've given you a bone. So now I'm going home," Franklin said as he started to gather up the books and notes and papers back into his school bag.

"I've given you a bone and now I'm going home. That's good," the big kid laughed, handing Franklin one of his books. "How'd you do that?"

"I just do," Franklin said, shrugging his shoulders, taking the book.

"Why don't you teach me," the boy said. "I want to write poems about titties."

"You'd have to go to the cities," Franklin said, zipping up his bag.

The big kid laughed, stood up and put his hand on Franklin's head and gave a playful shove. "You're okay," he said. "Yea, you're okay. See you around."

"Yea," Franklin said, slinging his pack onto his back. "See you around. Just don't hurt this little squirt, or grab his shirt . . . again. "

The boy shook his head, grinning, making a go-away gesture with his hand. "You're something else." The boy turned, and walked around the corner of the church.

Franklin grew three inches taller during that single school year, and the big kid never again stopped him to check his bag. The blue book had no more poems in it after that day, though Franklin had a way with words that the girls, still with smallish titties, found quite attractive.

14

Hawks Needs a Pass

"Mr. Hawkins, would you write me an A.P. and a H.P. for fifth period, so I don't have to go to band? I'd much rather work on the book."

Donald Hawkins flinched slightly, a little startled. He must have dozed off. He opened his eyes to see Melissa Brant. Both of Donald's feet were stretched out on top of the teacher's desk, hands behind his head, resting on the chalk board behind him. It was his free period.

He blinked rapidly.

"Jennie Dobbs is going to ask Mrs. Trent so we could work on it together."

Donald slowly pulled his feet off the desk, let his chair drop, and leaned forward on his elbows to study Melissa, a small girl with mousey brown hair in a crisp white blouse and a plaid skirt with matching suspenders.

"We did this last week," Donald said.

"I know, I know," Melissa started to plead. "I shouldn't have taken band. It was my mom who wanted me to do it."

Donald nodded his head, understanding. He didn't really give a damn. "A.P." was an "Alternative Project," which a teacher could write for a student to be excused from one class in order to give extra time for a particular project in another class. It had been instituted ten years earlier by a progressive superintendent—no longer with the district—who argued that learning was a fluid process that needed flexible boundaries. His idea was to allow the learner to flow with the moment's enthusiasm, to focus for an extended time on subjects of greater personal interest rather than being arbitrarily forced to attend to one disparate topic after another in a mechanical, clockwise fashion.

A good idea, perhaps, in theory. In practice, it opened the lid on Pandora's Box. Two years previously a committee had been formed to study its efficacy. Donald had no doubt that the findings would lead to the abandonment of the project, though it would take another couple of years. Some teachers prided themselves on how many students they could attract to extra time on their particular projects. Again, Donald Hawkins didn't really give a damn one way or another.

Here in Melissa's case, Hawkins knew that the band instructor— Gary Townes—would just as soon have the less talented, less enthusiastic members be absent. Many students used the A.P. pass to put in extra time at the band room.

"The book" Melissa wanted to work on was the Dawson Creek High School Yearbook, for which Donald was obligated to be Faculty Sponsor, since he taught the only two journalism classes— beginning and advanced journalism.

Donald studied the small girl in front of him and idly wondered if the production of the high school yearbook, for which she was assistant special events photos editor, would be one of the highlights of her life.

Donald opened his center desk drawer and took out two pads and wrote out the A.P. form and the H.P form, H.P standing for Hall Pass. "Here you go, Meliss."

"Thanks, Mr. Hawks. You're the best," Melissa said, reaching for the forms.

"Hawkins, Melissa. It's Hawkins, not Hawks."

Melissa giggled. "I know, I know, it's just that everybody calls you . . ."

"I know they do. But not to my face. It's Hawkins, Melissa. My name is Hawkins. Mr. Hawkins."

"Okay, sorry," she said, hanging her head. "And thanks. A bunch." She turned and left.

Donald wondered why it irritated him so, such a small thing. He now, just this moment, suspected it might have something to do with First Sergeant Harold

Blackstone, the 33rd Paratroopers division, who always called him Hawks. Hawkins did not have the rank or the maturity or the courage to correct him. This was the same First Sergeant Blackstone who had led him and seven brothers into a narrow back alley in Falluja, "looking for promotion and medals of valor," as the cynics on the squad described it.

And it was in that alley that Sergeant Blackstone and four of the other members of the squad ended their duty on earth, in a sudden explosion of what appeared to be an abandoned bread truck. Donald Hawkins, second to the last when entering the alley, upon seeing the truck, had worried about this exact possibility. But he dared not voice his concerns to Sergeant Blackstone.

The bell rang. Classroom doors opened and the halls were suddenly filled with hordes of chatting, squeaking, laughing, shouting adolescents. Donald Hawkins rubbed his eyes with the palm of his hands. His free period was over. Soon, they'd be pouring into this room. Once again, he felt as if he were walking again into that back alley of Falluja. Once again, he turned, preparing for the explosion. An involuntary tear came to his eye.

"Sergeant Blackstone, I need an A.P. Pass," he whispered, as the first of the kids blew into the room.

15

Lift Off

"Nobody called?" Brandon asked.

As soon as he said it, coming in the front door, down the hall to the kitchen, he hated himself for asking. It showed such childishness. Such neediness.

His mother, standing at the sink washing a pan, looked at him with apologetic eyes, shook her head. "Sorry honey." She stopped washing, watching him.

"No biggie," he said. He put the bag of groceries— milk, cheese, bread—on the counter. His mother watched. "If it's okay, I think I'll grab a nap."

"Sure. You go. I'll put those away."

"Thanks."

Brandon turned and left the kitchen. He didn't want to deal with his mom pitying him this way. He knew she had sent him to the store for groceries they didn't really need, just to get him out of the house, help him take his mind off these last hours.

Brandon was six foot four and weighed two hundred and thirty pounds, almost perfect for a defensive linebacker. Almost, except the fractured knee he'd suffered in the game against Syracuse in his junior year that had sidelined him for the rest of the season.

He'd come back fairly strong in his senior year, but he'd lost just a tad of his quickness, and, secretly, his confidence, his bravado. He'd spent his life, since age nine, as an obvious star at this game. At Alameda High school, he'd set records—most tackles, most interceptions—they'd almost won the state championship. He'd had his choice of full ride scholarships at four different schools. He'd chosen Ohio State, Division One of course. If he wanted to go pro, he'd have to play with the big boys. He'd made varsity halfway through his freshman season. He had the stuff.

After graduation, Brandon had been drafted in the last round by the Cleveland Browns. He was let go in the first cut during summer camp. The Miami Dolphins invited him down. He hung on with them until the final cut. His agent tried and failed to get him placed in the Canadian League. He sat out the season, still training, running, lifting weights, working in his Uncle's Specialty Audio store.

In the second year after graduation his agent arranged a try-out as a walk-on in summer camp with the Kansas City Chiefs. He had made it through the first two cuts and then let go on the final cut. And then Derek Bukowski, who had made the team as defensive linebacker, suffered a separated shoulder in the third game against the Denver Broncos. Brandon had been called back, spent the rest of the season with Kansas, but mostly on the bench. At the end of the season, his contract had not been renewed.

And so here he was, his third year after graduating from college. The Philadelphia Eagles had given him a physical, which he had passed, but for some reason, never clear, had not offered him even an invitation to try-out. His agent thought he might have a chance with the Tennessee Titans but they had signed a new graduate from Alabama instead.

Today was the last day for any professional team to add players to their roster. His agent was hopeful, but of course also had several other players he was trying to place.

Brandon went to his room, shut the door, laid down on the bed. Of course he didn't get any damn phone calls, especially on his home land line. He had his own damn cell. That's what Mickey, his agent would call, if anything turned up. Mickey wouldn't call his mom on the old land line. Stupid, stupid question. *Anybody call?*

Brandon hated that his whole life's happiness, fulfillment, even basic direction was dependent on someone else's decision, someone who didn't even know him, hadn't met him, just watches a few snippets of film, and judges him by last year's numbers on a page.

Laying on his bed, suddenly, for the first time since he was nine years old, Brandon saw he might really do something—*be* something—other than a football player. He had wrapped the football dream around him so tight for so long,--the money he'd make, the athletic power and grace and mastery he'd demonstrate, and then of course the glowing attention he'd receive. He'd be humble, when it happened. But first, he had to have it happen.

Now, for the first time, though of course he'd worried about it before, but now, he actually felt how he was going through that door—three years out of college, professional football was not to be his destiny. He had always assumed he'd play for a couple of years, and then have enough money to retire, and do whatever he wanted. What he wanted right now was football, another chance.

But maybe it was not meant to be. Actually, no *maybe* about it. Here this afternoon it was obvious: He now had to invent—he was *free* to invent—a completely new identity, a new direction, a whole new meaning for life.

Of course, he'd had doubts before, but they were doubts as to how the new football identity would manifest. Now, he saw, the identity around football was a false identity, even childish. For the first time, he could see that life was so much bigger than football. For the first time, he saw that his life had always been bigger than football. He had just ignored that very simple fact. He now felt free—truly free—to create a whole new life, with new meaning, new purpose, completely outside of football. The possibility felt fresh, powerful, almost magical. He swung his feet off the bed.

Yes, he didn't *have* to be a football player! He could do anything, *anything* now. He was finally free!

Brandon felt the phone in his pocket vibrate at the same time the ring tone broke the silence of the room. He lifted it to his ear. "Yo," he said.

"Bro, get yourself to Arizona," Mickey said. "You're going to be a Cardinal."

Brandon realized he'd already started to fly, even before the phone rang.

16

The Plan

Derick set the bottle of Bud Light and the Little Debbie cupcakes on the late-night convenience store counter. Derick had watched too much television.

His plan was to use the beer bottle to hit the clerk over the head when the clerk turned his back to make change. The way it happens on television, and in Derick's plan, the clerk would be knocked out, slide to the floor, and Derick would then jump over the counter, the cash drawer open, grab the dough, maybe some smokes, jump back over and make his escape.

That was the plan.

Derick had been glad to see that the clerk tonight was a scruffy middle-aged guy with a name tag that said, "Mark." Derick knew it had to be a guy for his plan to work. He couldn't hit a chick over the head with a beer bottle. A guy, yea. Chick, no.

Walking in, Derick, deep in his hoodie, (he figured cameras couldn't see his face if he had on his hoodie) had nodded slightly at the guy and then went to the cooler to get a single, long-necked bottle of Bud. The

The Plan

Little Debbie cupcakes were a spur of the moment addition to the plan.

Derick gave the clerk the ten-dollar bill he'd stolen from his mother's purse. (He'd put it back when the caper was over.) The clerk turned, opened the cash register. Derick grabbed the bottle by its neck, lifted it and came down hard, breaking it on the back of Mark's head, spilling beer down Mark's back.

"*Oww*," Mark squealed, as his shoulder blades instinctively closed in response to the cold beer down his back, and simultaneously Mark's hand went to the back of his head. He turned to look at Derick "What'd you do that for?"

This was not part of the script, not part of the plan. They stared at each other. "This is a stick-up," Derick finally said, pointing the now much shorter neck of the beer bottle at Mark. "Give me all the cash in the drawer. And give me my ten dollars back."

"Oh jeez, you idiot," Mark said, still holding the back of his head. "You'll never get away with . . ."

"Just give it to me," Derick said, pointing the bottle towards him.

"Okay, but there's not much here. We never leave . . ." he turned toward the cash register. His hand was bloody. "Look what you did!" he said, showing Derick the blood.

This wasn't part of the plan either. Derick looked around, saw the hot dogs turning over a spit. He stepped over and grabbed some napkins. He thrust them at Mark. "Just use a napkin," Derick said. "Don't get blood on the money."

Mark took the napkins, shook his head, cleaned his hand and put another napkin to the back of his head. He reached to the scotch tape dispenser on the counter, tore off two pieces and taped the napkin to the back of his head.

"Good idea," Derick said, about the tape. "And put the money in a bag." He hadn't thought about how to carry the money, but now that he had, he was proud of himself for thinking ahead like this.

Mark shook his head again, and reached for a bag under the counter, and of course pushed the button that alerted the police that a robbery was in progress.

"And put some Kools in there, too," Derick said.

"Kools? Mark asked, turning form the cash register.

The Plan

"Cigarettes, asshole," Derick said, pointing his bottle top as if it were a Luger. "Five packs, six packs. A lot of them. Put them in there."

"Okay, okay," Mark said, closing the cash register and reaching up and taking three packs of Kools and putting them into the bag with the money.

"I saw that. I said five. That was only three."

Mark reached up and took down two more packs of Kools and put them in the bag and handed the bag to Derick. Derick took the bag and looked in.

"Did you put all the money in the bag, including my ten?"

"Yes, I told you, we don't ..."

"I don't believe you, but it'll have to do, this time," Derick said.

And with that he dropped the long neck, now short neck bottle top on the floor, turned and ran out the door.

Mark, surprisingly agile, jumped onto the counter, swung his legs over and went after him.

Derick ran out the door, across the parking lot, across the street, into a vacant lot, Kool cigarettes falling from his bag. Not realizing he was being chased, Derick

81

slowed, and then was completely surprised when he was tackled from behind. Within moments, Mark was sitting on Derick's back, twisting his arm up toward his shoulder blades.

"Ow, ow, get off me, you fucker," Derick yelled, wiggling, trying to get free.

"Shut up, you idiot," Mark said, pushing Derick's head into the ground.

Flashing red and blue lights appeared in the convenience store parking lot.

"Over here, over here," Mark yelled. They heard him.

Derick's plan, cooked up while he was held in the local country jail, was to plead "not guilty." He had let his beard grow, shaved his head, and started wearing his grade-school glasses, which he had asked his mom to bring to him. Maybe Mark wouldn't be able to identify him for sure. And the coup-de-gras in his plan: Here in the jail, when allowed outside in the courtyard to smoke, he had switched to Winstons. That way, he could tell the judge, "I don't even smoke Kools." And he'd have witnesses to back him up.

A least that was his plan, so far.

17.

Basic Training

"Inner stillness is not about *not* having thoughts. Stillness is about not pushing forward. Not getting lost in your momentum. Willing to be right where you are."

"Right where I am is looking at five to ten years locked in this god-damn hellhole."

Arnold smiled at the young con named James. "All the more reason to practice stillness."

"Seems like stillness would make time drag even more, "James said. "I can't wait to get out of here."

"Just watch."

"Whadda you mean?"

"You say you can't wait. But here you are in the cage. You're waiting."

"And I hate it. Can't stand it."

"Because you are pushing against the bars."

"Hell yes. That's only natural."

"Not natural at all. Very common, yes. But not natural."

"Hell, they have us locked and chained like caged animals. It's only natural to want to get out."

Arnold nodded. "Best way to get out is to learn to be still."

"I see why they say you're a crazy old coot."

"If you had learned to be still while you were on the outside, you wouldn't be here."

"If I'd had any sense, I wouldn't be here."

"Exactly."

"I was drugging and thugging and living *la vida loca.*"

"Always wanting to be somewhere else, pushing forward, pushing, pushing, pushing."

James hesitated. "Yea, I guess so."

"Without learning stillness, you push yourself into the grave."

"Or prison."

"The suits are doing the same thing. Pushing, pushing into their own prison, towards their own grave."

"So tell me it again."

"Stillness isn't about not thinking. Stillness is about being willing to be just where you are."

"Ah hell, okay, I'll try it. What I've been doing sure hasn't worked."

Albert thought, yes, okay, he's passed the first test. He's a possible recruit, to help us break out. But first, his mind and emotions need training.

18

SEMI-RETIREMENT

Cliff sat on his wooden rocking-chair on the wooden porch of his small wooden hut, watching the two men wind their way up the mountain toward his retreat. He let out a long breath, while muttering something unintelligible with that same long breath.

Cliff was deeply aware that CIA agents never really retire, even though the papers are filed and the monthly pension appears in his bank account. That was just the surface story.

All agents, but especially case offers who conducted "special assignments," were like communist Chinese technocrats and diplomats who would serve in particular roles for a long or short duration and then "stand back"—but not stand away— to let the next party member fill the role. One of the advantages of single party rule was that after every election, those who had been replaced were not expected to fade away, but rather stick around and help the next official get a sense of the history and ongoing challenge of the position.

The CIA was definitely modeled after the "one party rule" system.

"We operate much more like the commies in Beijing than Washington bureaucrats," he told his old colleagues on more than one occasion. Both advantages and disadvantages to never being able to retire from the CIA.

The advantage is that one is always engaged, overtly or covertly, directly or indirectly, with various operations around the world. The complaint of many retirees that they no longer felt useful, no longer felt engaged, was not the case for CIA special operatives.

The stock and trade of the Agency, after all, was intelligence, in all its multi-hued expressions, but most particularly the human intelligence that comes with decades exploring the nuances of foreign cultures, foreign lusts and aversions, foreign expectations and surprises. Cliff was a walking foreign intelligence gold mine, with one hundred and ninety six countries on his resume. The Agency was not going to "retire" such a gold mind as long as the gold was so easily retrieved and so necessary for ongoing operations.

The disadvantage for not being able to retire from the CIA is that one is always engaged. And no matter how inconvenient one tries to make the "gold retrieval process," the CIA is ever up to the task.

"Howdy boys," Cliff said, when the two men finally arrived, a bit red-faced and panting at his mountain top—well, almost to the top—abode. He had not moved from his chair as they approached his cabin. "Fine day for a hike."

"You're now a fucking monk?" the older of the two men said, by way of greeting.

Cliff grinned. "Actually, Elaine, my dear woman companion, mostly prefers city-surrounds, so there's not a lot of fucking going on up here, though on occasion, when I'm in the city..."

"Jesus," the old man said, shaking his head. "Cliff, this is Isaac Bowman. Special opps, Damascus."

"Tough assignment," Cliff said, nodding his head at the younger man. "You must be good."

"How do you do, sir," Isaac said, stepping forward so he could shake Cliff's hand. Cliff half stood, shook his hand, then sat back down in his rocking chair.

"Really, Cliff. What the fuck are you doing up here," the older agent asked. "You're a gazillion miles from anywhere. The sign says this is a monastery. The blissed out hippie types down at the main lodge were protecting you like a sacred Buddha or something. Wouldn't tell us where to find you. Finally convinced your pony-tailed Abbot, but only after he had talked with the Vice-President of the fucking United States who convinced him that this was that important."

"The Abbot talked with the V.P.?" Cliff asked, grinning wide.

"Can we sit down?" the older man asked.

Cliff waved to the front porch, in front of his rocker. The older man sat. Young Isaac continued to stand.

88

"Stay there," Cliff said, and stood and went into his cabin. He came out in just a few moments carrying a silver tray with three glasses, a pitcher of water and a bottle of Johnnie Walker Blue Label, a bowl of ice. He obviously had prepared it as the two climbed the mountain.

"Jesus, Blue Label," the older man said. "When you go on retreat, you do it in style."

"Let's chill a bit, " Cliff said, "enjoy the view, the air, the peaceful mountain sounds, before we are forced to discuss your dirty little business."

The young man, Isaac Bowman, cocked his head, studying this revered old hand, this wizened new monk. Isaac generally didn't drink, especially during the day, but here he knew he should make an exception.

19

Soccer Drone Mom

"You can't go to work all day killing people and then expect to come home at night and be a loving soccer mom."

Teresa sipped her coffee and looked across the kitchen table at Jake, her ex. For the 10,000th time she thought, *Jake just doesn't get it* --- no, she didn't *think* he didn't get it. She *knew* with certainty he didn't get it. That's why he was her ex.

"Bite me," she said softly, and turned and looked out the window at the fading evening light of their backyard. Just because Jake didn't understand her work didn't mean he was wrong. She just didn't want to hear it right now.

Teresa didn't kill people every day. She killed people maybe once or twice every three months, at most. Often not a single enemy for months at a time. And only after intelligence had been cross checked, double checked and then triple-checked, and only when the target was at least 50 meters away from a compound of natives. Only when he, or she, was alone on a motorcycle, for instance, or hiding under a rock, would the kill order be given.

Soccer Drone Mom

Teresa was a Senior Surveillance and Prevention Technician on active duty with the Ohio National Guard. From their base outside Greenville, Ohio their unit controlled the overhead surveillance drones monitoring Kandahar Province in Afghanistan.

When Teresa, sitting at her controls in Ohio, had the target in her crosshairs, thanks to the powerful camera on her UAV—*unmanned aerial vehicle*, or drone--- she could push her button and, with a two second delay because of satellite transmission, an AGM-114 Hellfire Missile would be fired with deadly accuracy at whatever target was in her crosshairs. The computers that controlled the Hellfire missile were calibrated to adjust for the two second delay.

Only when a target was actively firing at US or allied forces, or was an immediate danger to US or allied forces, say from a rooftop, then the 50 meter distance regulation was suspended. It was understood that in such a case, the target brought on responsive firepower and was thus himself or herself solely responsible for any collateral damage that might occur. Such an incident had happened today. They had taken out a sniper, and the house he was using, near Baghi Pul Park in the old city. Collateral damages had been unavoidable.

Jake tried to be supportive, Teresa knew, but he just didn't understand the tensions and forces at play, both at home and abroad.

"If I didn't go to work every day, our family would be . . ." Teresa finally said, re-engaging the old argument . . .

"I know, I know, " Jake said, putting up his hand in a stop signal. He stood from the table, taking his cup to the sink. "I don't want to hear it."

Teresa was paid well for her work with the Guard, which also paid for health insurance for her and the kids. Jake had been laid off from the Mid-West Grains mill. This was one of the reasons he had moved back in. Teresa had invited him, even pleaded with him, pointing out how practical it would be, and the girls – – Jenny, age 12, and Heather, age 10 -- would love to have them back together again.

Her affair with the Colonel, which had been the outward cause of their breakup, had ended years ago. Although she had had several "quick flings," as she thought of them, with other colleagues, men who did understand her work pressures, Jake's persistent attention and tenderness to the girls and his tenderness with her in the kitchen and in bed was very attractive, and welcome.

Lost again in one of their verbal impasses – neither knowing how to carry the conversation back into safe territory — Teresa stared through the kitchen window into the backyard. Suddenly, at the corner of the window, she saw a movement . Something, someone coming over the side back fence, which was locked. Her heart skipped, then began to beat rapidly.

"Holy Jesus," she said to Jake, as she slid down to her knees, next to the kitchen table. Jake was rinsing his coffee cup at the sink. "Jake, get down! Get down! Someone's out there."

"What?" Jake said, standing at the kitchen sink, looking at Teresa crouched next to the table, now crawling under.

"For Christ's sake! Get down!" Teresa said. "Someone's in the backyard."

Jake put his cup in the sink as he sank to his hands and knees. "Where? When?" he asked in a whisper.

"Just now. I saw him come over the fence."

Teresa's team had recently had a secret briefing in which they had been warned that the Islamic State had issued a fatwa for the deaths of all drone operators. They had encouraged sympathizers to find where the operators live by checking phone directories and Facebook pages. When she had told Jake, he thought it was a stretch for Islamic terrorists to actually be here in Greenville, Ohio.

"You never can tell," Teresa had said. "Who thought they would be in New York on 9/11?"

Teresa crawled on her hands and knees through the kitchen to her purse in the dining room. She took out the SIG Sauer P229 pistol she had been issued. She carried it, still on her hands and knees , as she returned to the table.

There was a knock on the back door.

"God! Don't answer! Don't answer!" Teresa called, turning over and now sitting on the floor, pointing the gun at the back door.

Jake crawled to the back door and slowly stood.

"No, Jake!"

He inched the curtain away from the back window.

"No, Jake, don't..." Teresa called.

"Put it away, Teresa," Jake said softly then opened the back door. Ten year old Billy Nelson was standing on the back porch.

"Can Heather come out to play?" he asked.

Teresa, sitting on the kitchen floor, her Sauer pointing, hung her head and broke into sobs.

20

One Problem with the 2nd Amendment

Out of new habit and dark intent, Bennie reached out and quietly checked the driver's door of the big silver Dodge Ram truck. It wasn't locked. "Bingo!" he whispered, and smiled.

"Torson!" he whispered twice as loud. It was three a.m. His middle school buddy, Torson Abrams, was checking cars on the other side of the street, ten yards ahead of him. Torson turned. Bennie made six pointing motions to the truck door. Torson started his way and Bennie could see his crooked white teeth glowing in the moonlight.

Torson was having a sleepover at Bennie's house. After Bennie's mom had finally gone to bed, shortly after midnight, Bennie and Torson had crawled out Bennie's ground floor window, dressed in dark hoodies, to "go prowling," as they called it.

What they most enjoyed prowling for were window shades, or curtains, not completely closed, behind which they hoped to see ladies undressing for bed. They started this evening at 12:30 which was a bit late for such shades. Ten thirty to midnight was prime time. But tonight Bennie's mom had been caught on a television movie. She always checked on him before she went to bed. When he was alone, he and she would often exchange a few words, say good night, I love you, you too, that type of thing. Without fail, she would pull his blanket up around him, kiss him on the top of the head. Sometimes—more often these days— he would pretend to be sleeping. Still, she would smooth his blanket, and kiss him good night. He wondered–suspected – she knew he was faking sleep.

When he had a sleepover, generally with Torson, she would just pop her head in. Good night boys. Don't stay up too late. Tonight, when they heard the TV turn off both he and Torson pretended to be sleeping. His mom had simply opened the door, looked into the room lit only by the soft nightlight, then closed the door again.

Here at the truck, the boys knew the drill. When Torson arrived at the truck, Bennie opened the door, the cab-light came on and Torson quickly knelt down and pressed his thumb on the light button in the door frame making the truck go dark again. Bennie began rifling the truck's compartments— ashtray, door pockets, where people often kept spare change and even dollar bills. This cubbyhole was stuffed with receipts. The glove compartment was locked.

"Bingo!" Bennie said half flying across the front seat. "Hand me the persuader."

Torson pulled a small iron wedge out of his back pocket and handed it to Bennie. The wedge had come from Torson's dad's toolbox. The boys had learned that when the glove box was locked, it often meant real treasure inside.

It took a bit of effort for Bennie to pry the glove box open, but it finally did spring. When it did a Remington 380 pistol in its holster fell out onto the floor. Torson jumped back and the light came on .

Bennie said, "get the light! get the light!"

Torson knelt, pressed his thumb against the light button again. Bennie picked up the gun and holster. This was a first.

"Should we take it?" Bennie asked

"Fuck yes. Grab it, and let's get out of here."

For a long moment, Bennie hesitated. This was scary. His mom hated guns. He just assumed he did too. And he knew they were expensive. He wanted to put it back into the glove compartment.

"Come on, come on," Torson said again.

"What would we do with it?" Bennie asked. It was heavy and frightening in his hand.

"Big bucks, dude. Big bucks. And the guys will think we're cool. Very cool. Come on! Let's go."

Bennie held the holstered pistol and slipped back out of the truck.

"Let's vamoose," he said when standing in the street again. Torson let the light come back on and slowly and quietly closed the door. When the light went off again, both boys started running down the street.

As they ran, Bennie was thinking they shouldn't have done it, he should have stood up to Torson. These things are expensive and dangerous. He knew his mom didn't like Torson as much as she had liked some of his other friends, but she never said anything. A block and a half away the boys slowed and walked in the shadows.

"Let me see it," Torson said. Bennie gave it to him.

"Cool, very cool," Torson said, shaking his head up and down as they walked, taking the Remington 380 out of its holster. "We're big time now."

21

The Honker

The kid starts honking his damned horn as soon as he pulls into the loading zone, a few minutes after six every morning, six days a week. First a couple of strong beeps-- *bwaaat bwaaat*. Then, no more than a minute later, not long enough for anybody to answer the first honk, he lays on the horn.... *bwaaaaaaaaaaaaaaat. bwaaaaaaaaaaat. bwaaaaaaat.* It was driving me crazy.

He'd been doing it for almost a month, ever since he and his buddy Red got the construction job. I could just imagine him sitting inside his car-- a rusty old Chevy Nova-- grinning. If he had to be up, then everybody had to be up. *Hey look at us, we're worker men*!

Actually, the honking didn't wake me up. I'm retired, up by five, five thirty at the latest. Still, the honking bugged me. It showed no respect. No upbringing. No civility. Somebody obviously had to do something.

My backyard butts onto Thurston Boulevard, directly back of where the kid pulls up and honks. There are apartments across the street, where Red, his buddy lives. I've got a six-foot cedar fence, of course, across the whole of my back yard, and juniper bushes and cedar trees and whatnot, along with the roses, to try and cut the traffic noise. Everybody on my side of the block has the same six-foot fence. Thurston's a busy street.

I got the idea of what to do—a miniature catapult— from watching the history channel. I'm an old guy. I've been collecting odds and ends for forty years or more so I just had to ruffle around in the garage. I came up with a heavy spring and latch from an old gate, an old ladle, a gear off an old hand meat grinder, a broom handle, stuff like that. I have to admit, putting the thing together, I actually started whistling, grinning, feeling good.

When I finished, it was a work of art, if I do say so, about the size of an old-fashioned eggbeater, maybe a little larger. I attached it to the back of my fence, inside, just below the top, so when the arm of the catapult flung straight up, it was over the fence, but a second later, when it fell back, the way I'd rigged it, it was behind the fence, nobody the wiser.

Cars did not often park in the loading zone, where the kid pulled up in the morning, so it was easy to test out my contraption, get my distance, adjust. I kept an eye out and whenever there was an empty space I'd fling this little thing I'd made —the end of a sock with dirt in it, about the size and weight of an egg, tied with string. Since I don't have a gate onto Thurston, I'd have to walk from my fence back across my lawn, through my house, out the front door and around the block to cross the street and nonchalantly pick up the dirt sock. That's when I got the idea of a long twine attached to the trigger that I could pull from my house. And that led to rigging the twine all the way up to the second floor, my den, where I could watch the results.

I had to make a lot of adjustments, of course, using stronger twine and adjusting eye hooks, but I finally got the thing just right. All of this took me, start to finish, including adjustments, about four full days. But I was ready. And truth tell, they'd been about the happiest four days I'd had in years.

The kid pulls up 6:15 next morning. *Bwaaa bwaaa*. I was waiting. I pull the twine, fling the egg. Splat! Bulls eye. Driver's side window. The kid jumps out of the car. Slams the door, looking around. Everything's quiet. I'm upstairs, pulled back from the window, cackling like a mad man. My wife comes in. I zip my lip. She wasn't in on my plot. Wouldn't understand. "Nothing. Just feeling good," I say.

Next morning, same thing. *Bwaaa. Bwaaa.* I pull the twine. Splat! Perfect. The kid really lays on the horn now. *Bwaaaaaaaaaaaaaaaaaaaaaaa.* I laugh, I don't care. Kid gets out, looking around, mad as a hornet, swearing, m.f.'ing. Sees nothing.

Next morning's Sunday. They don't work Sundays. Monday morning, the kid shows up, parks a bit further back this time. One quick *bwaaa* on the horn. But that's enough. I pull the twine. Splat the hood.

This time, the kid gets out with a pistol and starts shooting up and down the block in every direction, including at my fence. Holy s.! I duck from the window, then crawl to the floor. Get flat, spread -eagled. The wife comes in again, stands at the door. "What's happening. What are you *doing*!?" she asks.

"*Get down, get down,*" I shout, on my belly, head turned to her, flapping my arm.

Long story short, police come shortly after the kid drives away, but people know who the kid is, he gets arrested at work, gets p.o'd at Red, doesn't come to pick him up any more. Nobody knows where the egg came from. I dismantle the thing that morning, right after the cops left. I didn't feel like sauntering over to add my two cents to what the neighbors were telling the police.

It worked out okay, I guess. Nobody hurt. They say a guy has to do what a guy has to do. But I didn't *have* to do that. Sometimes, just by plain dumb luck, a guy doing what he *wants* to do, just for fun, makes things better.

Truth told, the kid down the block with his loud music has me thinking about what might be done with those new little remote controlled drones...

22

An Insomniac's Tricks

"**M**aybe I drank too much," Bascom thought, his eyes open, staring at the clock, which read 4:18 a.m. Beverly, his wife of 33 years, was asleep in the other room—her room. They'd learned they both slept better with such an arrangement. Their sex life was good. Separate beds was about their sleeping life.

From his own perspective, Bascom didn't drink to excess. Occasionally a glass or two of wine with dinner, especially when out with friends, but regularly enjoyed a few Scotch "nightcaps" before bed. He'd read that this might be the cause of his current insomnia.

Whatever the cause, here he was, alone and awake in his bed hours before dawn. This was not a rare occurrence, so Bascom had picked up a few tricks to help him go back to sleep. His main trick, most recently, was to let the images of all the people in his life arise in his awareness—just long enough for him to repeat to himself, "love him," or "love her," and then move on. No analysis, no train of thought. Just a quick wave, or shout-out, as the kids these days say—"*love ya, love ya, love ya*" – to the neighbor, to his boss, to the trash man, to another neighbor. To his wife, his kids, coworkers, childhood sweetheart, store clerk, carry out boy. The trick was to keep the images moving, one after another.

Generally, employing this trick, he'd find himself waking up two or three hours later.

This morning, however, in the dark in the bed, the trick wasn't working. Usually, he could move from one image to another as easily as dealing cards from a slick new deck, one after the other. "Love him, love her," deuce, ace, images coming and going in a leisurely pace, as fast as he could deal, as fast as he could image another random person in his life.

In this particular pre-dawn darkness, for some reason, although the images would come, and he would quickly love them, bless them, the images would not disappear when he moved to the next. They were all jumbling up.

So now, laying here in the dark, all the people in Bascom's life, both present and past, important and not, seemed to be hovering over the bed. And, he had to admit, hated to admit, except for his wife and two kids, he didn't really love these people. He liked them, sure, enjoyed them, each in their way, a bit or a lot. But if one or another should disappear from his life, or had never appeared to begin with, would it really matter much?

Bascom briefly considered getting out of bed, here at 4:28 in the morning. Maybe sit in a chair. Meditate, read a book. But he continued laying in bed, considering the people in his life, now hanging around.

He realized—sensed—that in the same way his life would not change much if one or another were not there, family excluded, of course, so too, if he were not here, these people's lives would not change much, or at all, after the first drama of his disappearing.

"Maybe I drank too much," he thought again. "Booze, after its initial rush, drains my psychic energy. That why I feel no love, no *joie de vivre*."

He had an image of himself, laying alone in bed, alone in the world.

"Love him," he thought. "Bless him, poor old coot." He realized he really did love that guy, and his ordinary life.

He woke to the smell of coffee that Beverly had started. He smiled, the sunshine coming through his 7:25 a.m. window.

23

Henry's Wince

Henry winced as his wife Sheila turned down the potato chip aisle. The wince was sudden, involuntary, and unexpected. And Henry himself barely noticed. But his lips contorted in a grimace, his eyes closed and he gave a hardly perceptible shake of his head. His body momentarily turned, just slightly, muscles contracted, and then he relaxed.

Again, simply, Henry winced.

He was following Sheila around the store. She knew what they needed. She was pushing the cart. She knew what was where, and what was next. Henry was following, agreeing, adding what he could, which wasn't much.

Henry's wince, as she headed down the potato chip aisle, had more to do with the sudden memory of the words of Trudy Davenport, his secretary at work. Today Trudy had told Henry about Larry Dominick's complaint – Larry being Henry's and everybody else's boss—about this month's low production numbers.

Though good last month, this month Henry's numbers were among the lowest.

"Heads are going to roll, he said," Trudy had said.

"You want regular or barbecue?" His wife Sheila asked, standing in front of the Lays display.

"Regular, I guess," Henry said, "unless you want barbecue. Doesn't make much diff to me."

"Barbecue tastes like chemicals," his wife said, putting a family size bag of regular into their basket.

And again, Henry was both grateful and burdened by her job as a nurse at the local hospital. Her work was steady, necessary, unlikely to be either improved or threatened. They could almost make it on her salary alone, if need be. Almost.

Harry wished they could be done quickly with the grocery shopping. He wanted to be home, dinner over, sitting in his easy chair with a shot of Jack and a Coke, close at hand, TV or the paper or both also close at hand. Get his mind off things.

"Heads are going to roll," he remembered Trudy quoting that pig-head Dominick. Suddenly, the 10,000 items of the grocery store were too much.

"Sorry babe, I'll meet you in the car," he said. "I've had a really long day. I need to be outside a minute."

"Okay," she said. "We're just about done."

Just heading for the doors, not needing to check out, was a relief for Harry. Walking through the automatic doors, the cool air brought him back to earth. Harry breathed deeply, exhaled, headed for their Pontiac. He caught sight of Venus, on the horizon.

"Starlight, star bright, first star I see tonight," came automatically to mind. He wished he could think of a really good wish. He continued toward the Pontiac. His head probably wouldn't roll, he thought. He hoped.

24

The Star People Finally Showed

The star people finally showed themselves, clearly, openly, unmistakably on Armistice Day, November 11, 2041 at 11 in the morning Greenwich time. They showed simultaneously in 11 different world capitals. Their message began broadcasting across all media channels even before the ships showed themselves.

We come in peace with a small suggestion.

Of course, the earth jets were scrambled and land to air missiles employed over Washington DC, Jerusalem, Istanbul, Paris, Moscow, Buenos Aires, Beijing, New Delhi, Mexico City. It was Thimphu, the capital of Bhutan the only country in the world to employ a national happiness quotient, that did not try to shoot down the spaceships. The star people came and went all in less than ninety minutes.

Casualties did occur, unfortunately, and were particularly heavy in Washington DC, Moscow Riyadh, and Jerusalem, those countries' where heat seeking missiles suddenly found no heat being emitted from the invading ships so instead turned to F-16 fighter's futilely chasing the seemingly faster than light invaders.

The space people— who later identified themselves simply as elder cousins from a force field which we earthlings know as the dog star Sirius— never fired a single shot. Whether they even had weapons was a question never answered.

They simply showed themselves, in a dozen or more large and small ships, over each of the capital cities and then they let the chase begin. The jets and the missiles never came close, though as was counted later, tens of thousands of rounds had been launched at the invaders. The mere presence of these ships appearing in the forbidden airspaces had been interpreted by the military and political authorities as an act of war, or terrorist invasion, though, again, neither weapons nor threats were ever used.

On the contrary, communication via radio signals received in every capital, in the local language, assuring those on the ground, *we come in peace with a small suggestion.* Such assurances were of course ignored until it became quickly quite apparent that these ships were untouchable, indeed, untraceable, by any of the war technologies available to earthlings. Washington DC was the longest holdout, sending wave after wave of jets and missiles, creating havoc in the air and on the ground for almost an hour killing many thousands of their own citizens in an escalating barrage of firepower that went up and came down.

During the entire time, a message was being broadcast on every channel in every medium. *We come in peace. We have a small suggestion.* It wasn't long, of course, before ordinary people of the world became aware of what was happening. All radio and television channels had been commandeered and were broadcasting the events, the World Wide Web was live streaming, mobile phones were turned on via the emergency broadcasting system.

Simultaneous with the message, a wonderful, uplifting and soothing music was flowing through all the channels behind the repeated message, *we come in peace and have a small suggestion.* Some people, of course were panicking, running crazily through in the streets, where traffic lights were no longer working but simply flashing. The star people were getting the attention all at once of everybody on earth.

After an hour or so of demonstrating the utter failure of the earthly missiles and jet intercepts, the star people above Washington D.C. announced, "In 10 minutes we will land with our small suggestion in a cornfield outside of Des Moines, Iowa." They gave the exact coordinates. They likewise landed in the other ten countries, in ordinary, innocuous places similar to Des Moines. In the U.S., the local TV station set up its crew which coincidentally happened to be just 9 minutes away.

When they landed, a feminine voice came from the ship. "We have been watching you earth citizens and quietly helping to govern development for many thousands of years," the voice announced. "We can appear in whatever form is most appropriate or pleasing. For example . . ."

At that moment, a door lifted on the Des Moines ship and a tall, movie star like man and even more beautiful woman appeared in the doorway and smiled and waved at the television crew. "But on our home planet," the voice continued, "this is our natural shape." The movie stars gracefully shrank to the classic three-foot beings with big heads, small bodies and huge dark eyes.

"We come now, around the world, because if you don't change your leadership, you risk extinction," they said. "You have been a beautiful experiment and we don't want your extinction. The one small suggestion we have come to make is this: look for your leaders in shorter people. You continue to elect tall leaders, in your political parties and your businesses, because at one time big people were most useful for fighting large animals and invading tribes. But look what happens to tall animals—on your planet, dinosaurs and pterodactyl, elephants and rhino and manatees. They are going extinct. Physically large leaders are leaders of physical force. That's why they are so often sexually promiscuous. Our small suggestion is to look for smaller leaders.

"At this point this is just a suggestion. But that could change. You have witnessed our advanced technology. We will give you 20 years to begin to implant this process. We will watch and then we will show ourselves again. We would suggest 5'5" as the top height, to begin with. And yes, we recognize that at this time mostly women will be in this category. But your silly aberration of electing tall leaders will lead to extinction. We suggest small leaders."

And with that, all the ships all over the planet lifted gracefully into the sky and then, in a flash, disappeared.

That is how, *"Elect Ms. Shorty"* became a worldwide movement.

25

A Working Vacation

"Gladys, this is Mickey Belcher. He works for Gordon. Mickey, this is Gladys. She and I go way back. I mean, way, *way* back."

"Just quit, Thelma. We're not old enough to go way, *way* back."

"Don't fool yourself, Gladys dear. Mickey, Gladys and I go back to before either of us were married, for the first time, or divorced, or remarried, or widowed..."

"How do you do, Miss Gladys, from way, way back. Pleased to meet you. I was taking this drink-- it's a Manhattan-- to my companion, but I see from here that she already has a drink and you don't. Would you care for a drink?"

"Well, thank you, yes. If you're sure. That's very nice. I was just on my way . . ."

"Oh good, here, please. Now I won't have to return it, or drink it myself. You're doing me a favor, I assure you."

"That's sweet."

"Gordon says Mickey is always his man of the moment. Oops more arrivals. Can you two just chat while I go greet my guests?"

"Of course, Thelma love. This is your soirée, your anniversary. You go, your duties to perform."

"Just don't tell Mickey any of my secrets."

"They are safe with me."

"And Mickey so glad you could attend. Gordon will be so pleased. Coming all the way from Pittsburgh. Was it just for this?"

"This, and a little business. But mostly this. Wouldn't miss it."

"Thank you again. Got to run. Sorry. We'll catch you both on the turnaround."

"Go, Thelma. Go, go. We'll be fine."

"So, way, *way* back?"

"Actually yes. Sorority sisters. Omega Chi. Vassar."

"Wow. Vassar. I'm impressed."

"Don't be. It's amazing what daddy's money can buy."

"Still..."

"That was another life. Let's drop it. I wouldn't even be at this party if Thelma hadn't insisted. Said that Gordon insisted. What do you do for Gordon?"

"Human resources. Fairly boring, actually. Though it has its moments."

"Hiring and firing, that sort of thing?"

"Exactly. Though mostly firing these days, sorry to say, what with the economy the way it is. And you? Do you work?"

"Oh God no. Again daddy's money. And a fairly hefty life insurance policy, that I would have preferred not to cash in so suddenly, along with a company settlement..."

"My condolences. That's right, Thelma mentioned, widow..."

"Two years ago this June. You might remember, if you've been with the company, and are in human resources. Industrial accident, or so they say. Crushed in a trash-truck compactor."

"Oh yes, of course. Thomas Bolt. He was your husband? Such a tragedy. I'm so sorry for your loss."

"Being in human resources, you must have been part of the settlement paperwork."

"No, sorry. That's not my department."

"Not your department? You're not involved when a company employee ends up somehow comatose in a dumpster and a trash truck just happens to come by and empty the bin at 11 o'clock at night?"

"But didn't the inquiry find, forgive me for saying it, that he had been drinking, and drugs were found..."

"Tommy was a radical, but he'd become almost a teetotaler. He was a triathlete."

"Again I'm so sorry for your loss."

"So what do you do for human resources if you're far enough up the ladder that you fly in from Pittsburgh, but don't handle paperwork on an employee's accidental death?"

"The lawyers were quick to jump in..."

"You may know, Tommy found out something about Gordon's keeping two sets of books. I didn't want to come tonight. I still don't trust Gordon. But like she said, it's their anniversary and Gladys and I go way back.

I'm still trying to get someone to believe me. Jesus what was in this drink? All of a sudden I'm feeling... I'm feeling...

* * *

"What happened?"

"I have no idea. We were just talking about this crazy weather and then she said she wasn't feeling well and suddenly just dropped her drink and collapsed. Then went into those convulsions. I tried to help."

"My God I think she's dead."

26.

Glowing Winni

The first time Brother Winni went invisible he wasn't aware it happened. As Sister Cecilia—C.C. – started shouting, "*Oh my God, oh my God*," Winni slowly grew visible again.

"What's wrong?" asked Brother Arnie, who was leading the meditation.

"Winni, Winni," Cecilia said, jabbing her finger, pointing to Winni at the front of the small hall where the seven of us had gathered. "He wasn't there. He was there and then he faded away. I watched, I . . . I . . ." And then Cecilia fainted, and fell sideways off her cushion.

Winni was looking around dazedly, as if he had just awakened from a deep sleep.

"You okay, Winni?" Arnie asked.

"Sure," Winni said. "Why? What's happening?"

"C.C. fainted." Arnie stood from his own cushion and went toward C.C.. She rolled her head, moaning, coming back around.

The seven of us were in Valley View, a small A-frame that we'd turned into a meditation hall. When C.C. shouted, I was sitting near the cabin's back door. In addition to meditating I was tending the fire in the small wood stove.

Sister Pam held C.C.'s head with one hand and a water bottle to C.C.'s lips with the other hand. C.C. took a few sips, pushed it away, went up on an elbow and looked at Winni. Again she pointed, jabbing her finger.

"You disappeared," she said. "You just—just—it was so freaky. You started fading away, until you weren't there."

"I did?" Winni asked, clearly astounded.

"Yes. I was watching you, just because you looked so peaceful, so at ease and then . . . then, you started fading away. I couldn't believe what I was seeing, which was *nothing*. That's when I started shouting.. . . "   C.C. turned on her back again. "That was so freaky."

"It's okay, baby," Pamela said, patting C.C. on the shoulder.

"Winni, did you disappear?" Arnie asked.

"Well, sure, on the inside," he said. "But not . . ." Winni looked around at each of us, again, seeming somewhat stunned. And then he broke into a big grin, the one he's famous for. "I don't believe it," he said. "You guys are pulling my leg."

We all just stared at him, without a word.

"What was your meditation?" Arnie finally asked.

"Same as always," Winnie replied. "You know, moving attention to the formlessness within all form, the way the Abbot taught us. "

"Were you experiencing formlessness?" Arnie asked.

"Sure," Winni said. "Well, not me. The me disappeared. But formlessness itself was present, formless awareness."

"The me disappeared?" Arnie asked.

"Sure, " Winni said, a bit defensive. And then grinned wide again. "But no different than how you guys disappear." He looked around at us, nodding his head, as if looking for agreement.

"It's fun, right? We just disappear into the nothingness, just like we were taught?"

Sister C.C. fainted again. We all just stared at Winni, who was smiling and glowing, glowing.

27

A Brand New Game

Larry was new here.

That guy Finny had told him he should wait in line with the others, but then Finny left. Finny, was a pick-up player who Larry had met just this morning on the golf course. Finny didn't know that Larry had a lifelong aversion to waiting in line for anything. A lifelong quirk. This had always been a point of contention with Larry's wife, Alice.

"Oh Larry, it won't be that long," she'd say, maybe at the Red Lobster when told it would be ten minutes before a table was available.

"Not doing it," he'd reply. "Let's go." Larry could be a bit of a domestic bully.

So now, seeing the long line in front of the big white building he was told to wait in—who knew how long the line was inside the building—Larry decided he wanted to check things out first, get a sense of this new place that guy Finny had dropped him off in. Maybe the line would go down while he went exploring. The weather was perfect.

Just a few hours before Larry had been playing golf with Finny and two of his regular buddie but now here he was. They hadn't even let him finish his golf game. He was feeling very anxious, very uncertain about the whole affair. Not exactly sure where he was or how he got here. Waiting in that line would have been hell for him.

Over the hill, in the opposite direction, Larry thought he saw green pastures, or maybe even a golf course. If they actually had a golf course here, maybe things were looking up. At least golf is something he was familiar with, knew a thing or two about.

"I don't know if you should leave," said the short scrawny guy in a baseball cap at the back of the line that Larry had been talking with. Larry had asked the guy what the line was for—but the guy was just as new as Larry. The guy guessed it might be some kind of entrance review, but he wasn't sure.

That's when Larry decided he'd go check things out for himself, not stand in line.

"Better to ask forgiveness than permission," Larry said, waving over his shoulder to the scrawny guy, without looking back.

Larry followed a very gentle winding path to the top of the hill. When he reached the top, he saw yes, by gum, it was a golf course. Flags flying, small groups of men and women playing. Looking at the course, Larry saw it was so big, disappearing into the distance, it was at least eighteen holes. In fact, there might be two courses here, side by side. Wow. That would be wonderful.

Since they had come for him when he was at his usual golf course back home, Larry was still dressed in his golf clothes—shoes, pants, shirt. He grinned big and headed for the greens.

Suddenly, he found himself in the clubhouse, a big, beautiful, post and timber club house, the desk up front, men and women golfers moving in and out, talking, laughing, some apparently just finishing a round, some ready to go. Larry was a bit stunned, and confused. Larry didn't remember—couldn't remember—walking from the top of the hill down to here. But here he was, nevertheless. Larry worried he was starting to have memory lapses.

"Hey there, stranger," a young man said, walking up to Larry and patting him briefly on the shoulder, as if they were long lost friends. The young man looked vaguely familiar but Larry couldn't quite place him.

"We need one more to fill out our foursome," the young man said. "You interested?"

"I don't know," Larry said. "My first time here. What are the fees? I'd have to rent some clubs. Left mine back home. I'm really, really new to this place.."

"Fees are covered by your membership," the young man said.

"I don't think I'm a member," Larry said.

The young man laughed. His teeth were very white and straight, highlighting his smooth, tanned complexion. "You're here, dude. That means you're a member. If you weren't you wouldn't be here."

"I was supposed to wait in line," Larry said, pointing a thumb over his shoulder. "But I left, and came here instead, so maybe . . ."

"Perfect," the young man said. "That means you're truly one of us. Let's golf. Follow me." He turned and started walking out of the clubhouse, toward the greens, pointing in front of him for Larry to follow. Larry followed.

The next thing Larry knew he was in his sister Virginia's living room, where much of his and her family – nieces, nephews, cousins—were gathered. His sister was sobbing. His brother-in-law was patting her shoulder.

"But he wasn't saved," she sobbed. "He played golf every Sunday morning, almost to spite Alice, who was so faithful." She sobbed even harder.

"Hey, Ginny, Ginny, sis, it's okay, it's okay," Larry said. "I'm here. I'm okay." He didn't know how he went from the golf course to here so quick. Things weren't quite adding up.

"The ways of the Lord are beyond comprehension," his brother-in-law said, still patting Ginny.

"Hey, you guys, you guys, I'm here" Larry said more forcefully. But no one heard. His cousin Louise walked right past him, seemingly right through him on her way to the kitchen for another brownie.

"He'll be okay," Louise said, patting Ginny on the knee as she passed.

"Hi Uncle Larry," his three-year-old great-niece Alexandra said, standing in front of him, looking straight up at him. "Everybody's really sad about you," she said. "But here you are. So they don't need to be sad any more, do they?"

Larry shook his head in agreement. "No, they don't," he said. "You tell them. I'm fine. I'm playing golf."

"Yo, dude, you ready to tee off?" the young man said, softly taking his elbow.

Larry was surprised and again a bit confused, to find the young man by his side.

"I guess so, yes," he said to the young man, glancing again at the roomful of relatives.

"Great," the young man said, and Larry once again found himself standing next to the green pastures, golf clubs nearby, on what appeared to be hole number one for a brand new game.

28

Life Changing Questions

Billy Vandermot didn't even want to open the damned envelope. Seeing who it was from – Anderson Auto Credit—he knew what it was going to say. He opened it anyway, to see how much time he had.

Billy had just come home from work. He was still in his work clothes, still had his coat on. It was 9:30 p.m. He was a custodian at Travis Moss elementary school. His work day started at 2:30 in the afternoon. He'd finished up early today,

His apartment was a mess—he needed to wash the dishes, do his laundry, pick up the papers in the living room, open some of the other mail he had tossed on the coffee table. It was nice to be home, but it didn't feel much like home anymore. He needed to get his act together. He'd be thirty in just two years,

The letter started with a lot of legal mumbo-jumbo. He skipped down He just wanted to know how much time he had, and how much he owed..

$12,538. 87! What the hell?

He had borrowed $14,000 and he had been paying on it, $188.68 a month, for three and a half years.

Sure, he had missed a payment or two, had gotten behind, paid late a couple of times, and was late again this month, but geez! He still shouldn't owe that much.

Billy had put $750 down on a four-year old Nissan Rogue Sport. The $750.00 was all that the insurance company had paid for the Honda he had totaled when he slipped off the road one icy night coming home from work. The Honda had flipped onto its top. Billy was lucky to get out alive, though he came out without a scratch. Well, he did come out with a scratch—a welt—across his chest, from the seat belt. But that healed within two weeks.

Billy still owed $2,980 on the Honda. He didn't want to think about that.

December 15th. Ten days before Christmas. They actually wanted Billy to bring the damned car back to the dealership show room on or before that date. Either that or pay the $12, 538.87 in full. When he brought it back, they would be willing to pay him $7,350.00 for it. Their own damned car. Leaving him still more than five grand in debt to them, but without a car, which they'd sold him for $14,750. Now here three years later they would give him only half of what he'd paid for it. After he had made all those payments!

And besides, how was he supposed to get home if he took the damned car back to the dealership?

Billy threw the letter on the kitchen table.

He plopped into a kitchen chair, closed his eyes and let his head fall back against the door jam. He wanted to cry. But he wouldn't, of course. How could he get out from under all this?

He let out a deep breath, opened his eyes, stood up and removed his coat, hung it on the back of the chair.

He went to the refrigerator. He still had a piece of the pepperoni pizza he had ordered two nights before. He'd been eating a lot of pizza lately. And convenience store gas station food—hot dogs and burritos and chips. He put the pizza slice directly on the microwave turntable and hit "one minute."

He knew he should put the pizza on a plate and cover it but the microwave was already so dirty he'd have to clean it up or get a new one here soon—one more pizza slice won't make that much difference.

As he ate his pizza, at the paper cluttered kitchen table, Billy thought about calling his dad, just to connect with someone who knew him and loved him. Billy's dad was even more broke and more in debt than Billy himself. His dad had lost his driver's license—too many DUI's—and his dad's girlfriend's car was the only car they owned. His dad rode his bike or took the bus to the garage where he worked part time. They paid him under the table. His dad was very proud of Billy, and Billy's job,

129

which came with benefits and paid holidays and vacation. His mom had died when Billy was six.

There was a knock on Billy's apartment door. That was very unusual. Billy walked across the living room and opened the door. A short, stocky man with a flabby face and wearing a brown leather jacket was standing in the hall with some papers in hand.

"William Vandermot?" the stocky man asked.

"Yes?"

The stocky man held the papers out. Bill took them. "Sorry to say, friend, you have just been served with a summons to appear in court. Your car company wants their money back."

"Which car company?" Billy asked.

The stocky man shook his head, turned, walked away, holding up a hand. "Good luck, buddy." He stopped and turned around in the hall.

"Are you a lawyer? " He waited a moment and then answered his own question. "No, you're not a lawyer. Maybe you should be. You need one. I hate what these people are doing to kids like you. Maybe you should go to law school. Somebody should stop them. Good luck, son."

The short stocky man turned and walked away.

Billy looked at the papers. "Lots of legal mumbo jumbo," was his first thought. And then, his second thoughts were questions, "Get a lawyer? Go to law school? Could I be actually be a real lawyer?"

Thirty years later, sitting in his wood-paneled den drinking his nightcap Singleton scotch, a new Mercedes parked in the garage, Judge William Vandermot for some reason remembered that late night process server, and raised his Waterford glass in gratitude. Judge Vandermot did not each much pizza these days.

29

Far from the Madding Crowd

"**M**ister Hippi Researcher, can you see there's not enough room in this valley for the both of us?"

The big man in the dirty cowboy hat sat tall in his saddle, holding his Winchester rifle across his lap, the large black horse making the man's presence even more ominous.

Luke looked up at the man in the saddle, and then slowly looked off to the right. As far as he could see was open valley grass land, outlined in the blue hazy distance with the majestic snowcapped peaks of the Wind River. Just as slowly, Luke moved his head back left, stopping to look up at the man for a long moment, then continued to the left as far as his head would turn. Again, the horizon seemed fifty miles away, nestling empty rolling hills. Luke slowly looked back at the big man on the horse, again pausing to stare at him..

Then Luke again slowly turned and looked behind him, where his camper was parked in the shade of tall cottonwoods, the only vehicle nestled in the campground next to the river. Luke slowly looked back and up at the man on the horse.

"Not enough room?" he asked, smiling.

The man in the cowboy hat shook his head, leaned over and spit a wad of tobacco juice that landed close to Luke's tennis shoe. Luke stared at it, then looked back up to the cowboy.

"See," the big man said. "You're crowding me."

Again there was a long pause as the two men studied each other.

"I'm legal," Luke said in a quiet voice. "I've got the permit. Researching the black footed ferret. Endangered, you know. "
The cowboy slowly shook his head, spit tobacco juice over the other side of his horse.

"Like I said, not enough room out here for me, you and your so-called research," he repeated. "You be crowding me." The man lifted his rifle, cocked the hammer handle.

"I be crowding you?" Luke asked, smiling. He stared up. "Are you aware you just used a grammatical construction originating in the urban African American culture, a construction which linguists would classify as Ebonics? They'd be both delighted and surprised to find your clever usage here in rural Wyoming."

The cowboy furled his eyebrows? "What?"

"The traditionally accepted grammatical construction for the sentence you just uttered would be, 'You *are* crowding me.' When you instead employed the third person normative and said, 'You *be* crowding me,' you adopted a form of phrasing which has its origin in the urban black culture, often employed to demonstrate difference and even conscious disrespect for the

133

oppressive white culture and its traditional linguistic imperatives."

The cowboy looked at the young man in disbelief. He aimed his rifle to the right and fired at the ground. Luke flinched. "Dance you fucking hippie." The cowboy put his rifle on the other side of the horse and shot again.

This time the horse frightened, whinnied, rose suddenly on its hind legs. The movement threw the cowboy back, and he spontaneously pulled hard on the reins with one hand, trying to stay on. He accidently shot a third time into the air. The horse, feeling the reins and startled again by the third shot, turned suddenly and fell on its side. The cowboy's hat flew off. He dropped the rifle. As he and the horse hit the ground he yelled, screamed in pain. The horse shivered and quickly stood again and immediately began to run toward the far mountains. The cowboy lay on the ground, writhing, holding his leg.

"Think my goddamned leg's broke," he groaned.

Luke slowly went over and picked up the rifle. He then went over to the man and looked down at him.

"Yep, I think so too," he said. The man groaned again, wincing in pain, looking up at Luke with his mouth open.

"Fortunately," Luke said calmly, turning his head first right then left. "There's plenty of room out here for a broken leg."

"What?" the cowboy asked.

"But since you asked so nicely, I guess I'll just leave." He turned and started slowly towards his camper.

"No wait, don't go," the cowboy called.

Luke didn't turn around, walking slowly, knowing he'd have to drive his camper back past this cowboy, to the top of the far hill, which was the nearest place he had found for cell phone reception. He'd let the cowboy enjoy his own wide open space, until the sheriff and ambulance would arrive.

30

Safely Into Syria

The heat was making all of us cranky and lazy.

We were sprawled out with our battle rattle next to the tarmac under shade awnings that had been erected over dry brown grass. Five hundred grunts, waiting, in Texas. Again.

In Texas the sun doesn't bounce off glass or chrome, like it does back home in Saginaw. In Texas the sun's so hot it just hits and sits, then slowly oozes up in heavy, lazy waves so gravy thick a fellow could stretch out his hand and pull back a gob of sticky heat, if he had spunk enough to stretch out his hand. I didn't have that much spunk.

"You think it's hot here," Staff Sergeant Hendrix said, "you ain't seen nothing yet. Wait til we get to Doha. Right, Hanson?" He looked at me from ten grunts away and giggled. I didn't say anything. Hendrix is an idiot, apparently in charge of morale boosting.

We were at Fort Hood, in Killeen, Texas, waiting our turn to be loaded into the C-140 transports, flying to Camp Doha Ad-Dawhah, north of Kuwait City and then on to Bombaconda--- Baghdad Airport and the Sandbox. Nevertheless, being from Michigan, Texas itself was hot enough. On that day everybody thought Texas was hot enough.

It's central Texas towns like Killeen and guys like Hendrix, that give Texas and the army a bad name. In Killeen, if you get off post—which any sane man would want to do—nothing's there. The town's squatty, dirty, paint peeling from the hot Texas sun off shabby one story houses, nothing fancier than a k-mart or a kentucky fried, main street lined with car dealers hawking fast wheels at high prices to soldiers wanting to get to Houston or Dallas or San Antone, anywhere but there. And it's hot, stupid hot, almost all the time.

When I first signed up as a kid in Saginaw I envisioned myself wearing a spiffy uniform with hero ribbons. I envisioned dancing my nights away in, say, France, where the girls wear no underpants. Or maybe I'd be in Spain or Tokyo or somewhere else exotic and sinful and fun. Or maybe just plain ol' Fort Ord, California dreaming. My recruiter, a friendly guy named Al, helped with such visions. He suggested that's how it'd be, after I'd done my obligatory stint in Iraq.

Yea right. When I signed up as a kid I was expecting to go to Iraq, willing to do my part, help out where I could. But this would be my third time back. I wasn't a kid any more. My visions of army life had been deeply tempered by reality.

Laying there that day under the awning, I thought back about my basic training and then studying radar repair in windowless rooms in metal buildings. Days and months of being herded into noisy chow halls where we ate off metal trays, put up with racist jokes, cranky red necks, suffering night after night in barracks with farting meat whackers. I thought sure it had to get better. Then two tours in the Sandbox, almost back to back, with the heat and the blood and the stupid, stupid decisions by suck ups who didn't seem to care that we –all of us, whether we're soldiers or *hajis*—were all human beings. And the absolute worst— days in the heat standing guard at the crossroads, not knowing what was coming next, scared as shit. Radar repair. Yea, right.

And now here I was heading back, again.

Our turn finally came. "Okay girls," Hendrix said. "Here we go." We stood up, grabbed our rattle— our packs, rolls, all the crap we carry—found our places in the squad line. Déjà vu all over again. We walked out from under the sun screen, across the tarmac, towards the same C-140 that had been sitting right there for the last two hours. Single file, heading for the belly of the beast, with the sun like a magnifying glass on the top of our skulls. And that's when it happened.

Suddenly, from out of nowhere, I felt a cool breeze, as if it was spring in Saginaw.

Safely into Syria

I stopped. I didn't want to miss it, or walk away from it. I didn't want to get into a plane where I couldn't feel this breeze.

I definitely felt it. It was cool, sweet, like back home again. I even caught the scent of the delicate pink Dragonmouth flower that grew near our lake front home.

Jason Karswell, first man behind me, ran into me.

"Jesus, Hanson. What you doing?" he asked. "Get a move on."

But I couldn't. I wouldn't. It was as if I just woke up. The sweet cool breeze was blowing across my neck, my face, soft and easy. Images came back of when I was a kid on my uncle's farm in the spring, swinging in a swing under the apple tree, feeling the cool breeze under my arms, smelling the sweet blossoms, singing happy cowboy songs. Again, there on the tarmac, in that breeze, it was as if I suddenly woke up.

I looked around and suddenly realized where I was, and who I was, and what I was doing, and what I was about to do, and what I had to do instead. There would be no breeze inside that troop carrier. There on the tarmac, I took a deep breath of the cool breeze, smiled and then just sat down.

I couldn't do it again. Wouldn't. I knew that the kid under the tree back in Saginaw wouldn't do what I was about to do. Not again. Not a 3rd time. The real me wouldn't do that again. The real kid just would not get in that plane.

Sure, the pretend-me who played at being a soldier with hero medals to spare could do it, easy. The soldier-me, following orders, could, if I let it, yank the kid-me up by the neck and tell me to get a move on. That soldier that was in me could just stand back up, apologize, make up an excuse—sorry, it was the heat— then keep walking. That would be easiest. But the real me, the kid- me who had just woken up, just couldn't do it. Wouldn't. I would not play the soldier game any more. I would not walk away from the kid I was, the man I am, the man I want to be.

"Hey Sarge," Karswell shouted out. "Hanson's down. I think we got a problem."

"What's wrong, there, Hanson," Staff Sergeant Hendrix shouted, moving my way. "Heat getting to you?" Still sitting on the tarmac, I slipped the pack off my back.

"No Sergeant. I just realized I've had enough. I ain't going back. I quit." Even though Hendrix was there, I was saying it to no one in particular. The cool breeze picked up.

"I think he fainted," Karswell said, as the sergeant came up. "He just had to sit down. Maybe sun stroke."

"No, I'm fine," I said to nobody in particular. "At last. I'm just fine. I'm cool."

"Come on, Hanson. Get your butt up and move," Sgt. Hendrix ordered. He kicked at me a little.

"No sir, sergeant," I said, leaning back on my pack, as if I were under the awning again. "This is it. As far as I'm going."

"What are you talking about?" the sergeant asked.

The cool breeze continued to blow. Not since I'd left Saginaw had I been this comfortable.

"I'm just not going," I said again.

A different type of heat started at that point. A type of heat I could put up with, accompanied with that breeze. A type of heat that made me stronger, prouder, brave. I could feel the real man in me waking up, gaining strength as the court martial unfolded.

# # #

For several weeks, every night in my dreams in my bedroom in Saginaw, my nephew, my wonderful little Billy Hanson, would appear. I'd see him standing at a crossroads in the desert. And I would see a family of Iraqi's coming his way, in a beat up old Taxi cab. And I'd see Billy—Billy listening to the soldiers around him and, the loudspeakers blaring, not knowing what to do. In my dreams, I knew Billy was trying to decide whether to fire on that taxi cab. And then he does, and then he sees what he did, and the look on his face.... For several weeks, I would wake up crying.

I prayed for Billy, every night, that he'd stay cool, stay cool, not fire on those people. Every night, I prayed, that my little nephew stays cool. And then I started to pray, also, for those in the taxi cab.

And now I hear they have Billy in the brig. The dreams have not returned.

# # #

In her dreams, Mashib sees her nephew, Ubra'm, driving his mother, and sisters and their neighbors' daughter, out of the city, to safety. In her dreams she sees them approach a border crossing, where a young blond- haired man is standing with an automatic rifle. A loud-speaker is blaring, and the blond solider shouts something, but Ubra'm does not hear, wants to get closer to show the soldier that he is harmless, that he is only carrying women. The young blond solider hesitates, and then fires into Ubra'm's car. Mashib wakes up crying, sweating. She often dreams this dream, and then wakes crying, sweating. She prays for Ubra'm, and the young women. And lately, she started praying, too, for the young blond soldier. That his mind stay cool. She prays that this bad dream will not let this happen.

This morning, she hears that Ubra'm made it safely with the young women into Syria.

31

Mission Accomplished

After spending half an hour cleaning up his workbench and hanging up his tools, Waldo Henderson, coffee cup in hand, stood at the top of his driveway, just inside the garage, studying his street and suburban neighborhood. Since his retirement, this pleasant evening puttering had become somewhat of a ritual. Waldo's wife, Melinda, was inside, reading a mystery.

Waldo gave a small wave at the lady walking her dog on the other side of the street. She passed their house almost every evening. They had never spoken, but had exchanged many such waves. As usual, the kids four houses down were out in the street with their bikes and skateboards, making excited kid noises. His neighbor two houses in the other direction was mowing his lawn before the sun went down.

Suddenly, watching this peaceful scene from this very familiar vantage point, Waldo realized that his driveway—this driveway—had the exact same slant, the exact width and same distance from the street to the garage as his childhood driveway growing up in the suburbs, seventy-five miles to the south down Interstate 25. Waldo was stunned. Living in this home for thirty-five years, raising his kids here, taking out the trash, shoveling the walk, mowing the lawn, he had not once realized that he had the same driveway—and by extension the same home, almost the same life—he had when he was young.

"Wow," Waldo said out loud, looking at his neighborhood with completely fresh eyes.

When he was a boy, Waldo's old man, Waldo Senior, used to hit and grab and violently shake him and his brothers for the least infraction, or no infraction at all, at least from his and his brothers' viewpoint. They never knew when the next punch would be coming. And when arguing with Waldo's mom, Henrietta, Waldo Senior would also grab and shove and pinch in a way that would make her cry and bruise badly.

Unlike many other violent fathers, Waldo Senior's violent temper was not the result of excess drink. His work, never steady, was as a public relations man. Waldo Senior's persona out in the world was of a happy, light-hearted man, ever-ready with a funny quip or polite, even obsequious compliment. Out in the world, he was a glad-hander.

His family knew better. Only at home did Waldo Senior's dark, demanding, frustrated and irritable character show itself through regular violence and irrational responses.

Waldo and both his brothers had left home as soon as they could, returning only seldom to visit their mom. Soon after the boys left home, Waldo Senior and Henrietta moved to a condo in Florida, where after ten years Waldo Senior died of esophageal cancer. Waldo Junior went down to help out his mom in the old man's last days. He and the old man never did hug.

"Wow," Waldo said again, here at the top of his evening driveway, as if just now waking up to his place here in the suburbs. For most of the years of his adult life, Waldo had a recurring nightmare, that he was back in his childhood home, either as a kid again, or, more often, as a grown man, forced to move back into their childhood home again with his own family. He'd awaken from these nightmares and be immediately grateful he was no longer there, no longer forced to live in such un-loving conditions, such an unhappy house.

Waldo loved his own home. In their back yard they had four bird feeders, a water fountain, rock garden, flowers, hammock. In the front yard, a swinging love- seat hung from the large limb of a honey locust tree that he himself had planted thirty-two years ago. Friends and family and neighbors came and went for dinners and card games and various communal projects. And he loved this, his garage, his workbench, garden tools, radio.

Mission Accomplished

Holding his coffee, thinking of his old man and the atmosphere of his childhood home, he realized his own suburban life's work had been just this: to bring peace to this environment. To go beyond the violence and frustration, the un-love to be simply glad for all that is.

Waldo recognized that he, himself, and this home itself was the penultimate evolutionary accomplishment: a man easy and at peace in his own skin and in his own home, in the evening of his life, on good terms with his kids and his wife and his neighbors, the workbench straightened, the lawn mowed, God in Her heaven and all's right with the world.

A neighbor's dog, free of its leash, ran frolicking down the street, children laughing and running after. Waldo spontaneously giggled.

"Melinda," he told his wife when he went inside. "I think you might be right. Maybe it's time we move to Portland, closer to the kids."

Melinda looked up from her mystery in surprise and joy.

ABOUT THE AUTHOR

Bear Jack Gebhardt is a "householder monk" at Heart Mountain Monastery, Nunnery and Art Colony, and the organizer of the New Buddhist Methodist Church, while still spending a bit of time as Head Coach at the Smokers Freedom School.

Bear is married to the artist, Suzy Summers Gebhardt. They have two grown children and two growing grandsons. He spends most days putting his attention on what he loves, and encourages others to do the same. He loves to read, write, hike in the nearby mountains (both alone and with friends), tweak his stock portfolio, lunch and dine and play poker with both old and new friends and oh yea, as often as possible, do his part to foment non-violent revolution, striving to bring more political, economic and spiritual power back to ordinary people.

See Amazon author's page and/or:

www.heartmountainmonastery.com

www.newmethodistchurch.com

www.beargebhardt.com

Other Books by Bear Gebhardt

- *How to Graduate from the Electoral College: A Layman's Plan to Regain Voter Sovereignty*

- *How to Stop Smoking in One Easy Second—A Heart Mountain Monastery Murder Mystery*

- *Confessions of a Two Timer: How to Use an Ordinary Kitchen Timer to Find Flow, Overcome Procrastination, Win Prizes, Be Popular and Become a Neighborhood Buddha*

- *A Wave of Thanks: and Other Human Gestures: 31 Quick Stories*

- *The Smoker's Prayer: The Spiritual Healing of Tobacco Addiction, with or without Chantix, Nicotine Patches, Hypnosis, Jail Time or Duct Tape*

- *The Potless Pot High: How to Get High, Clear and Spunky without Weed*

- *How to Stop Smoking in 15 Easy Years: A Slacker's Guide to Final Freedom*

- *Practicing the Presence of Peace*

- *Happy John: An Advaita (Non-duality) Gospel*

- *How to Help Your Smoker Quit—A Brave and Happy Strategy*

- *The Enlightened Smoker's Guide To Quitting*

- *Now Hiring: Finding and Keeping Good Help for Your Entry Wage Jobs* (With Steve Lauer)

www.ingramcontent.com/pod-product-compliance
Lightning Source LLC
Chambersburg PA
CBHW070334130626
46556CB00007B/2855